Final Swipe

By
Tory Swedlund

Table Of Contents

Chapter 1

Sarah drummed her fingers on the steering wheel, waiting for the school bell to ring. She glanced at the clock - 2:55 PM - just five more minutes until her daughter Emma emerged from the large brick building. The parking lot was already buzzing with activity as other parents arrived to pick up their kids.

Sarah's mind wandered as she watched the other mothers chatting happily together. Ever since her divorce last year, she had immersed herself fully in her career and in caring for Emma. Her days were busy, filled with back-to-back meetings and carpools and ballet classes. But sometimes, like now, she felt a pang of loneliness creep in. A longing for companionship.

The piercing ring of the bell jolted Sarah from her thoughts. Kids began pouring out the front doors in a chaotic stream. She scanned the crowd until she spotted Emma's dark head bobbing along, chattering excitedly with a friend. Sarah waved and Emma broke into a grin, skipping over to the car.

"Hey sweetie, how was school?" Sarah asked as Emma clambered into the backseat, throwing her backpack next to her.

"It was good! We did a science experiment and I got to light the Bunsen burner. It was so cool; the flame was all blue and hot!"

Sarah smiled, pulling out of the parking lot. Emma chatted happily about her day as they drove to her piano lesson. Sarah treasured these conversations; Emma's animated spirit never failed to lift her own.

After piano, they stopped at a trendy new cafe downtown to meet Linda. Sarah checked her watch as they sat down, noting Linda's habitual five-minute lateness. Right on cue, Linda breezed in, perfectly coifed as always.

"Sorry I'm late!" she was thrilled, embracing Sarah. "The salon appointment ran over."

Linda and Emma exchanged enthusiastic greetings - they adored each other. Once Emma was settled with an iPad game, Linda turned to Sarah, eyebrows knitting together.

"So, tell me how you're doing. Any new prospects on the horizon?"

Sarah knew what she meant. Linda had been trying to set her up on dates for months now.

"No, no prospects," Sarah said lightly, scanning the menu.

"Sarah, I'm worried about you," Linda said gently. "I know how. focused you are on Emma and work, but you deserve to find love. again."

Sarah shifted uncomfortably. "I'm not sure I'm ready to put myself out there again..."

"But online dating makes it so easy now! No pressure, just see if you connect with anyone. Won't you at least consider it?"

Sarah hesitated. Linda did have a point - it was time to dip a toe back into the complicated waters of romance.

"Alright," she conceded slowly. "I'll think about it."

Linda clasped her hands excitedly. "Wonderful! Let me know if you need any help setting up a profile. Ooh, this is so exciting!"

Sarah laughed, Linda's enthusiasm breaking through her reservations. She felt a nervous flutter in her chest at the possibilities in store. This would lead to another shot at love... Sarah smiled at her friend's enthusiasm but could not help feeling uneasy.

"I don't know, Linda," she said hesitantly. "The idea of putting myself out there on some app...it just seems risky. I mean, how do you know who you are meeting?"

Linda nodded sympathetically. "I get it, believe me. But so many of my friends have met great guys online. It's not like the old days of random chatrooms anymore - the sites work to make meaningful connections now."

She leaned forward, her voice earnest. "And just think about how convenient it is - you can get to know someone from the comfort of your couch, without having to coordinate schedules or find babysitters. It lets you screen people and make sure you're interested before you even meet up."

Sarah bit her lip. She had to admit, it did sound easier than trying to meet people in person.

"Plus," Linda continued, "you get to be picky! Do not feel pressured to swipe right on just anyone. Only chat with men you're genuinely intrigued by."

Sarah felt her resistance wavering. Linda had always been a trusted advisor. And it was not like she was asking Sarah to do anything crazy - just try a new way of connecting in the modern world.

"You think I could find someone special this way?" she asked quietly.

Linda grasped her hand, eyes shining. "Absolutely. You are an amazing woman, Sarah. You deserve a partner who can keep up with you. Let me help you put yourself out there."

Sarah took a deep breath and squeezed Linda's hand back, decision was made. "Alright, let's do this. I'm ready to take control of my love life again."

Linda cheered, and they laughed together, Sarah feeling lighter than she had in months. This was a leap into the unknown, but with Linda's help, she was willing to take the chance.

Sarah pulled out her phone, her heart beating faster. This was happening - she was taking the plunge into online dating.

"Okay, let's find you a good app," Linda said, peering over her shoulder. "How about Hinge? I've heard great things."

Sarah nodded and downloaded the app. Her stomach fluttered as she began setting up her profile. She chose three of her best photos. - one glamorous black and white headshot, one candid of her laughing in a sundress, and one of her hugging her daughter.

For her bio, she thought carefully. She wanted to come across as fun yet sincere. After a few drafts, she landed on:

"Mom to an amazing 7-year-old girl. I like checking out new

restaurants, theaters, and impromptu dance parties in the kitchen. Looking for a partner-in-crime who's kind, adventurous, and up for anything."

She showed the profile to Linda, who grinned. "I love it! Not too serious but still capturing your essence."

Sarah giggled. "Well, here goes nothing!" She uploaded the profile and officially joined the world of online dating. It felt scary yet thrilling, like peering over the edge of a high dive.

"I'm so proud of you," Linda said, giving her a quick hug. "You've got your feet wet - now it's time to start swimming in the dating pool. Do not forget to have fun with it!"

"I'll try," Sarah smiled. With her friend's encouragement, this leap of faith suddenly seemed not just possible, but exciting. She was ready to see what surprises the online dating world held in store.

Sarah took a deep breath and began swiping through profiles on the app. There were so many options - outdoorsy guys, intellectual types, rugged athletes. She focused on the ones that made her laugh or seemed genuinely kind. After about 20 minutes of swiping, she had made a few matches.

"Hey there beautiful, how's your day going?" messaged a handsome man named Matt. He seemed nice enough.

"Great, thanks! Just getting my feet wet with this online dating thing," she responded.

"Haha, I remember those days. Lemme know if you have any questions!" Matt replied.

Sarah smiled. This wasn't so hard - just friendly conversations. She matched and chatted with a few other men, keeping things light. Though she was still nervous, it felt empowering to take control of her romantic life.

Later that day, Sarah met Linda for coffee.

"So... give me the scoop! Any interesting matches so far?" Linda asked eagerly.

"A few nice guys so far. I'm keeping conversations casual - asking about their hobbies, interests, stuff like that."

Linda nodded. "Smart move. Have you thought about safety when you eventually meet some of them?"

"Definitely," said Sarah. "I'll make sure to meet in public, let you know where I'm going, and share my location on my phone."

"Excellent. You've got to look out for yourself," Linda advised.

Sarah agreed. She was venturing into unfamiliar territory, but with sensible precautions, she could navigate it safely. This was just the beginning of her journey, but the thrill of new possibilities awaited.

Sarah took a deep breath as she walked into the trendy wine bar. She was meeting Matt, a guy she had been chatting with on the dating app for a week. He seemed intelligent and kind - she was hopeful this could lead to something more.

Glancing around, she spotted him at a table, looking just like his photos. He stood up and waved, flashing a warm smile.

"Sarah! Great to finally meet you in person," Matt said as they hugged briefly.

"Likewise!" Sarah replied as they sat. A waiter came by for their drink orders.

The conversation flowed easily as they discussed their careers, hobbies, favorite books, and travel destinations. Matt had an energetic charisma that put Sarah at ease.

After an hour, Matt said, "How about we get out of here? A walk through the park?"

Sarah hesitated briefly, then remembered her safety precautions.

"I'd love that," she responded. They left the bar and strolled through the nearby park as the sun set, casting an amber glow on the pond.
Matt slipped his hand into Sarah's. It felt comforting and exciting all at once. For the first time in years, Sarah felt that spark of

possibility.

As they said goodnight, Matt kissed her cheek. "I had an amazing time, Sarah. Let's do this again soon?"

"I'd like that," Sarah replied, smiling. She watched him walk away, her heart fluttering.

The date exceeded her expectations. Though it was just a first step, Sarah felt hopeful about what lay ahead. The world of online dating was full of difficulties, but she was ready to embrace it with an open mind and heart.

Sarah sank into her couch, reflecting on the whirlwind of dating experiences since creating her online profile. Though she had her fair share of lackluster dates, there were also pleasant surprises like Matt that re-ignited her optimism.

Online dating opened possibilities that Sarah never imagined just a few months ago. With a simple swipe, she could connect with compatible singles she would have never met organically. The convenience of setting up dates from her phone was undeniably liberating.

At the same time, Sarah was mindful of the need for caution. She always let a friend know where she was meeting someone and made sure to meet in public places first. A few men had quickly revealed themselves to be untrustworthy, reminding Sarah that there were risks beneath the tantalizing surface.

While she was thrilled by new adventures like salsa dancing with Antonio and stargazing with David, Sarah was careful not to get swept away too quickly. She wanted to keep a level head and listen to her intuition.

With so many options at her fingertips, Sarah was determined to be selective and not settle. Her priority was meeting someone who could truly enrich her life and be a caring partner.

Though the path ahead was sure to have twists and turns, Sarah felt ready. Her outlook was hopeful, yet realistic. She knew the world of modern dating would challenge her in ways she couldn't yet imagine. But she was confident that with courage and wisdom, she could navigate it successfully.

Sarah smiled, feeling grateful for how far she had come. This was just the beginning, but her journey into online dating had already expanded her horizons. She was excited to see what lay ahead.

Chapter 2

Sarah's thumbs danced across the screen of her smartphone as she eagerly downloaded SwipeRight, the hottest new dating app. Creating a profile was quick and painless - just a few photos highlighting her warm smile and sparkling eyes, a witty bio, and a sincere summary of what she was looking for in a partner.

"Let the swiping begin!" she whispered under her breath, a rush of excitement swelling in her chest. Sarah settled onto the couch and began flicking through profiles, curiosity lighting up her hazel eyes with each new potential match.

Some men boasted of high-powered careers and exotic travel photos that seemed more glamorous than genuine. Others appeared kind but too meek for her taste. She lingered on a rugged mountain man whose passion for the outdoors aligned with her own before finally swiping left. For now, the thrill lay simply in the looking and imagining, like a voyeur peering hopefully into unknown lives. The world of possibilities swirled at her fingertips.

Sarah's stomach fluttered with butterflies as she gave herself one last glance in the mirror before her first SwipeRight date. She had chosen her favorite black dress, classy yet alluring, and added a touch of mascara to make her eyes pop. "You've got this," she whispered, psyching herself up.

She arrived at the trendy wine bar early, securing a table with a view of the door. Sarah sipped a glass of Cabernet to calm her nerves. Right on time, a tall man with kind eyes and a warm smile walked in and glanced around. Their eyes met - this was him.

"Hi, I'm Sarah," she said, extending her hand as he approached the table.

"Mark. It's so nice to meet you in person," he replied. His firm handshake exuded a quiet confidence.

The conversation flowed easily as they discussed their shared interest in hiking and travel. Mark had a profound sense of humor that kept Sarah laughing all evening. Under the dim lights, she felt an undeniable spark of connection.

For the first time in ages, Sarah's thoughts drifted away from work and motherhood. She felt like herself again - a vibrant, desirable woman with passions of her own. The world of online dating suddenly seemed full of promise.

Sarah smiled as Mark told a story about his recent trip to Peru, but something didn't seem quite right. He mentioned hiking the Inca Trail to Machu Picchu, describing the amazing views and remote villages along the way.

"That's incredible that you were able to get away for that long of a trek," Sarah said. "Don't you run a busy consulting firm?"

Mark's face flickered imperceptibly. "Well, it was just a short section of the trail. I wish I could've done the whole thing."

As the evening went on, Sarah noticed other subtle inconsistencies. Mark portrayed himself as an avid reader, but when she mentioned her favorite novels, he struggled to connect. He name-dropped people and places like he was trying too hard to impress her.

A nagging feeling started gnawing at Sarah. Mark had exaggerated parts of his profile to appear more adventurous and intellectual. She knew online dating could bring out people's insecurities. Still, the arrogance of his half-truths disappointed her.

Sarah's thoughts drifted to her daughter asleep at home with the babysitter. This man sitting across from her was a stranger. If she couldn't trust the basic facts he presented online, what else was he hiding? The world of online dating suddenly seemed full.

of risks and unknowns. She would need to proceed much more cautiously for the sake of her child.

Sarah sighed deeply as she swiped left and right on the dating app, barely glancing at the profiles flashing by. After two weeks of frenzied matching and messaging, the initial thrill had faded into a dizzying blur of names, faces, and mundane opening lines.

She clicked on yet another message popping up in her inbox - "Hey beautiful, I'd love to take you out this weekend ;)" Ugh. Delete.

The rapid-fire pace of app dating was starting to wear on Sarah. Keeping up with multiple conversations at once felt akin to juggling while walking a tightrope. She could barely keep track of who said what or discern any authentic personality behind the endless pickup lines and flattering filters.

When her phone dinged with another new message notification, Sarah groaned and tossed the phone onto her couch in exasperation.

"I need a break," she muttered under her breath.

Just then, her best friend Linda breezed into the living room, arms overflowing with takeout bags from their favorite Thai restaurant.

"Uh oh, I know that look," Linda said, depositing the food on the kitchen counter. "Date overload?"

Sarah nodded wearily as Linda joined her on the couch.

"I don't know, Lin," Sarah sighed. "Online dating seemed fun and exciting at first, but now it just feels...pointless. I can't keep all these guys straight, and I'm not connecting with any of them."

She hesitated, thinking of her daughter asleep in the next room.
"Plus, meeting all these strangers online...it doesn't feel as safe as I thought. I'm worried about the risks, especially with Emma to think about."

Sarah turned to her friend. "I know you encouraged me to try this, but...what if I just can't make it work as a single mom? Maybe I should give up on dating for now."

Linda wrapped a comforting arm around Sarah's shoulders. "Don't give up hope yet," she said gently. "I know it feels overwhelming, but you're smart and strong. We'll figure this out together."

Sarah managed a small, grateful smile, glad for her friend's reassurance. With Linda's support, she felt ready to step back, re-evaluate her approach to online dating, and proceed with greater wisdom. Her daughter's safety had to come first before any quest for romance.

Sarah took a deep breath, feeling resolved. "You're right, I'm not ready to throw in the towel just yet. But I do need to be more careful."

She grabbed her laptop, began to research safety tips for single-parent dating. Making a profile private, taking it slowly, and doing background checks were a few suggestions.

"I should meet in public places first, and tell Emma these are just friends, not introduce them as dates," Sarah murmured. She jotted notes, compiling a checklist to protect her child while exploring new relationships.

Returning to the dating app, Sarah scrutinized each profile - claims of wealth or perfection now seemed suspect. She asked pointed questions, probing for truth beneath the superficial.

One man eagerly offered his address "to pick her up" for their first date. Sarah hesitated, then firmly suggested meeting at a restaurant instead.

She sighed, wishing for a genuine connection but remaining guarded. With newfound wariness, she vowed to filter each interaction through the lens of what was best for Emma. Her daughter was and would always be her priority.

Sarah sat back on the couch, closing her laptop with a soft click. The past few weeks of online dating had been a whirlwind - meeting new people, trying to balance her desire for connection with protecting Emma. She was exhausted.

"Maybe it's time for a break," she mused. The constant swiping, chatting, and first dates felt like a second job on top of parenting and her career.

She thought about Emma, who was staying at her grandmother's that weekend. Her daughter's smiling face and infectious laugh filled Sarah's mind. Emma was the light of her life, her reason for being.

Sarah knew deep down that no suitor, no matter how charming, was worth compromising her child's well-being and sense of security. She needed to step back, re-center herself, and approach dating from a place of discernment rather than desperation.

Picking up her phone, Sarah opened the dating app and deleted her account. The relief was immediate - like setting down a heavy bag she'd been carrying for miles.

Closing her eyes, she made a silent promise to herself and to Emma. She would focus on being the best mother possible. When the time was right, she would try again - slowly, selectively, with wisdom to guide her. She had faith that one day, perhaps when Emma was older, the right partner would come along.

For now, Sarah just needed rest, time with her daughter, and the inner stillness that comes from listening to one's deepest truth. She was ready to close this chapter, but not the book. Somewhere on the next page, her story would continue.

Chapter 3

Sarah stirred her morning coffee, staring absently out the kitchen window. The rising sun cast a golden glow across the backyard, where dewdrops still clung to the grass. She should have felt at peace in this moment, but her mind was troubled.

She thought back to those first giddy conversations with Dave, the clever banter and flirtatious innuendos that hinted at a real connection. She remembered the flutter of excitement she felt each time a notification popped up on her phone, signaling a new message from him. For a while, the possibilities seemed endless.

But then came the night she waited eagerly in the restaurant, dolled up in a new dress, only to receive a text 45 minutes late that he couldn't make it due to a work emergency. The next day, a friend showed her Dave's dating profile, still active with recent photos. At that moment, the fragile trust Sarah had built came crashing down.

She stared into her coffee as if the dark liquid could divine answers to her swirling doubts. The betrayed optimism stung deeply, more than she cared to admit. Dave was not the first—there was Rob, who ghosted after three dates, and Mark, whose charming persona hid a controlling streak. Each left her more guarded, more cynical about the authenticity of any bond formed online.

Perhaps she was being naive, too willing to see the best in people instead of heeding the red flags. Or this digital realm allowed men to adopt false identities, conveying anything they wished without repercussion. Either way, Sarah wondered if she could ever lower her defenses enough to find real intimacy in the virtual world.

With a sigh, she pushed back such gloomy thoughts and headed upstairs to rouse her daughter for school. There would be time to unravel this knot of contradictions. For now, life called her to pour cereal, pack lunches, and nurture the one person she knew she could trust.

Sarah watched her daughter Lucy chatter away about her upcoming field trip as they ate breakfast together. She smiled at the girl's enthusiasm, but her mind inevitably wandered back to her dating predicament.

Part of her yearned to find a partner to share life's joys and burdens. Someone to greet her after a long day, take weekend strolls in the park, and one day walk Lucy down the aisle. But the bigger part recoiled at the thought of exposing her child to strangers who might charm their way into her life, only to disappear or worse.

She had seen other single moms rapidly cycle through boyfriends, eager to find a replacement dad. Sarah refused to rush into anything, determined to protect her daughter's stability and safety. But the loneliness crept in some nights, reminding her of all she was missing.

Lost in thought, she barely noticed as Lucy finished up and scampered off to brush her teeth. Sarah sighed and started clearing the table. She wished there was an easy answer, a way to find companionship without jeopardizing the life she had built. But nothing worthwhile ever came easy, she mused.

For now, she would proceed with cautious optimism. The world was full of possibilities, both beautiful and dangerous. She simply had to trust her instincts to navigate between the two. With a deep breath, Sarah steeled herself and headed off to take Lucy to school. This was her priority today. The rest could wait.

Sarah sat at her computer, steeling herself before logging into the dating app. She had taken a break after the last few lackluster conversations but felt ready to try again.

The first profile that popped up was Darren, 38. His pictures showed him on hikes, at bars with friends, and on a ski trip. He seemed active and sociable. After exchanging pleasantries,

The conversation took a flirtatious turn that made Sarah uncomfortable. When she tried to steer it back to getting to know each other, Darren disappeared.

Next was Zach, 44, a teacher. He complimented Sarah's smile and asked thoughtful questions about her job and life as a mom. But soon his texts became increasingly frequent and needy. Sarah gently explained she needed to focus on work and Lucy right now. Zach reacted angrily, accusing her of leading him on.

Shaken, Sarah took a break. She wanted to believe there were good men out there. But these encounters kept reinforcing her doubts, making her question if she was cut out for online dating. Every time she began to let her guard down, something happened to violate her trust.

Part of her wondered if she was being too cautious...too quick to find fault. But she had a responsibility primarily to Lucy. She couldn't ignore red flags or give men the benefit of the doubt like when she was young and single. Her child's safety had to come first.

With a weary sigh, Sarah logged off. She would try again another day, hoping her luck would change. But a voice inside whispered that she was searching for something that didn't exist - romance without risk, trust without doubt. Until she silenced that voice, she would remain on guard, proceeding with eyes wide open.

Sarah sighed as she set her phone down, the screen still glowing from her latest disappointing text exchange. She needed advice from someone she trusted, someone who would give it to her straight.

She dialed her best friend, Jenny.

"Hey girl, what's up?" Jenny said brightly.

"Ugh, I just can't figure men out," Sarah groaned. "Online dating is making me crazy. I keep meeting guys who seem great at first, but then they turn out to be jerks or just want something casual."

Jenny made a sympathetic noise. "I know it's frustrating, but you can't let a few bad apples spoil the whole bunch."

"I'm trying not to, but I feel like my trust is just being stomped on repeatedly," Sarah said.

"Well, only you can decide if it's worth it to keep trying," Jenny said gently. "Maybe take a break for a bit, then dip your toe back in slowly."

Sarah nodded, even though Jenny couldn't see her. Her friend made a good point - she needed time to clear her head before making any major decisions.

After they hung up, Sarah thought about calling her sister Amanda too. Amanda always gave blunt, no-nonsense advice. She dialed her number.

"Hey sis, what's going on?" Amanda said.

Sarah quickly explained the situation.

"Ugh, men," Amanda said bitterly. "That's why I gave up on dating years ago."

"I don't want to give up," Sarah said. "But I feel like I can't trust anyone."

"Well, you shouldn't trust them right away," Amanda said firmly. "Go into it with your eyes open. Don't ignore red flags just because you're lonely."

Sarah sighed. "I know, I know. I just don't want my past to make me too closed off, you know?"

"Look, you've been hurt before, but you can't let fear rule your life," Amanda said. "Just be smart. Listen to your gut. You'll find someone worthy eventually."

Sarah felt bolstered after talking to Amanda and Jenny. Their advice gave her a lot to think about. She knew deep down she wasn't ready to give up on love yet. But she also had to protect herself - and Lucy.

Curled up on the couch, she thought about her hesitations. Were they reasonable, or were her own insecurities and doubts holding her back? She wanted to believe there were still good men out there, men who would accept her and Lucy as a package deal. But she knew there would always be risks in opening her heart.

With a deep breath, Sarah resolved to move forward, but even more cautiously than before. She would listen to her inner voice and not ignore red flags. When the time was right, she would try online dating again. But for now, she needed time to rebuild her sense of trust - in herself and in love.

Sarah decided to take a break from online dating. She was feeling overwhelmed by the sheer number of profiles, messages, and potential matches. It was just too much information to sift through.

She also couldn't shake the nagging doubts about all the dangers that lurked behind the screens. Catfishing, ghosting, married men pretending to be single - she had heard so many horror stories from friends. And after her last experience of being lied to and betrayed, her trust in strangers had been shattered.

As she sipped her morning coffee, Sarah contemplated whether she should delete her dating profiles entirely. Maybe this whole online dating thing just wasn't right for her. She missed.

the old-fashioned way of meeting people organically through friends or at social events. It seemed more authentic. But she also knew she didn't get out much these days between work and caring for Lucy.

With a sigh, Sarah opened her laptop and pulled up the dating sites. Her finger hovered over the "Deactivate Account" button. But then she hesitated. Despite the pitfalls, there was a lot of potential in online dating too. Hundreds of eligible singles that she'd never otherwise met were now at her fingertips. She didn't want her doubts and bad experience to completely close her off from new possibilities.

Just as she was about to deactivate, a notification popped up. A new message from a man named Brian. He seemed sweet and down-to-earth in his profile. Nothing flashy or suspicious. Brian's message was thoughtful and asked interesting questions about her interests. Intrigued, Sarah clicked on his photo. He had warm, kind eyes and a nice smile.

Maybe she would give it one more chance, just to see if Brian might restore her faith. While the risks were real, Sarah knew she couldn't let fear stop her from trying to find love. She had to balance caution with openness. With a deep breath, she started typing a reply to Brian's message.

Sarah's fingers hovered over the keyboard as she contemplated how to respond to Brian's message. Part of her wanted to engage enthusiastically, hopeful that this could be the start of something real. But the other part remained wary, not wanting to let her guard down too quickly after being hurt before.

She started typing a friendly but measured reply, keeping details about herself and Lucy to a minimum for now. Sarah knew she needed to take things slowly this time, not rushing into sharing too much too fast as she had in the past.

After sending the message, she leaned back in her chair, conflicted about whether she was doing the right thing. Doubts crept in about her judgment in getting involved with

someone new. What if Brian was not as kind as he seemed? The stakes felt so high now with Lucy to consider too.

Sarah gazed at a photo of her daughter on the fridge, feeling the weight of responsibility. She wanted Lucy to have a complete family, but not at the expense of safety. It was a balance she struggled to find.

With a sigh, she turned back to the computer screen, rereading Brian's message, and her reply. The excitement of connecting with someone new mingled with trepidation. But she knew the only way forward was with cautious optimism, keeping one foot grounded while slowly opening her heart to trust.

Sarah closed her laptop, the screen going dark as she contemplated the path ahead. Though part of her wanted to dive headfirst into this new possibility with Brian, she knew restraint was needed. It would be so easy to get swept up in the thrill of it all, but she had to stay level-headed.

Walking over to the window, Sarah looked out at the neighborhood street below. Kids rode bikes while parents gardened and washed cars. Such a picturesque scene, yet she felt uncertain about where she fit in.

Turning back to the room, her gaze fell on a framed photo of Lucy. Sarah's heart swelled with love and fear - hope and doubt entwined. She wanted her daughter to grow up whole, with a loving family, but it had to be the right fit.

With a deep breath, Sarah steeled her resolve. This was uncharted territory, but she would proceed with cautious optimism. Eyes wide open for red flags, but heart open to possibility. She knew there would be twists and turns ahead, but she was ready for the journey.

Sarah picked up her phone, typing out a text to her best friend. "I've got a good feeling about this one but taking it slow. Wish me luck!"

She hit send, knowing that no matter what happened, she had her close friends to lean on. The future was uncertain, but she was ready to find out what held next.

Chapter 4

As Sarah Martin's cursor hovered with trepidation over yet another disappointingly banal dating profile, the pixels on her laptop screen seemed to mock her quest for companionship with their sterile glow. Her heart, once buoyant with the prospect of digital courtship, now sank like a stone in the murky waters of online matchmaking. The cacophony of trite conversations and ill-fitting matches had become a Sisyphean task, each encounter rolling back down the hill of her expectations just as she neared the peak of hope.

It was amidst this constellation of disenchantment that our narrative lens shifts focus, settling upon the visage of Tom Spencer—a single father much akin to Sarah in his digital endeavors. His short brown hair, trimmed with the precision of a man who values both time and appearance, offered a hint of the meticulousness that spilled into other facets of his life. The beard, well-groomed and edged, lent him an air of sophistication, not enough to intimidate but sufficient to suggest a man who has navigated life's tempests with a steady hand.

Tom's eyes, those revelatory windows to the soul, were soft with empathy, indicative of nights spent consoling nightmares and days filled with the laughter of children. His face bore the subtle signs of sleepless nights and early mornings—hallmarks of parental devotion and entrepreneurial aspiration intertwined. In these features lay a charm that was not of the flamboyant variety, but rather a quiet allure, the kind that whispers promises steadfastness and understanding.

The local coffee shop, a microcosm of urban solitude carved out in the heart of the bustling city, was alive with the symphony of clinking cups and indistinct chatter. An olfactory tapestry is woven from the earthy notes of freshly ground beans mingled with the sweet undertones of pastries, creating an aromatic allure that seemed almost tangible. Jazz melodies, subtle and unobtrusive, meandered through the air, wrapping patrons in a soft auditory embrace that complemented the café's warm palette and the gentle hum of congeniality.

Amidst this convivial backdrop, Sarah Martin crossed the threshold, her presence momentarily punctuating the atmosphere like a comma gives pause to a run-on sentence. The confident gait she had honed over the years seemed to falter, giving way to an uncertainty that made her steps tentative, almost reluctant. Her eyes, dark and incisive, darted across the room, not with the casual sweep of a regular patron, but with the precision of a hawk seeking its quarry amidst the camouflage of everyday café-goers.

In the quiet theater of her mind, skepticism took center stage, delivering a soliloquy that voiced her disillusionment with love's modern machinations. Yet here she was, a digital-age Penelope weaving and unweaving her tapestry of hope. A surreptitious glance at the reflection in the glass pastry case presented a woman who, despite the armor of a well- tailored career, now fidgeted with the hem of her blouse—a silent echo of her inner hesitance.

A hand rose, ostensibly to brush away an invisible strand of hair that dared mar the calculated casualness of her shoulder-length tresses, but in truth, it was a stalling tactic—a momentary respite in which she could gather scattered thoughts like a gambler rake in chips, steeling herself for the next round. The adjustment of her jacket's lapel followed suit, an inconspicuous attempt to reclaim some visage of poise in the face of vulnerability's looming specter.

She had arrived as Sarah Martin, the single mother whose resolve had been tempered in the crucible of life's vicissitudes, yet beneath that façade stirred the perennial human yearning for connection, for the intangible spark that might just transform the mundane into something extraordinary. And so, under the watchful gaze of the coffee-scented gods and amid the muffled soundtrack of life's unscripted play, she waited for Tom Spencer to emerge from the sea of anonymous faces and, perhaps, chart a new course on her digital map of the heart.

Amidst the din of caffeinated chatter and steam wands whistling like distant trains, she discerned him—a solitary figure in the corner whose demeanor cast a quiet oasis in the tempest of urban hustle. Tom Spencer sat there, his short brown hair a testament to meticulous grooming, and the well-tended beard lending him an air of refined masculinity that was at once inviting and slightly intimidating.

The moment their gazes intertwined, a metamorphosis transpired; his eyes, twin beacons of welcome in an often indifferent sea, ignited with recognition and warmth. It was as though the very act of seeing her dissolved the barriers of digital anonymity, and Sarah found herself momentarily adrift in the unexpected candor of his smile.

"Sarah?" he ventured, his voice threading through the hum of activity to reach her, rich with an authenticity that set loose a flutter of relief within her chest.

"Tom," she acknowledged, allowing the name to anchor her as she approached, her surprise at his genuine amiability evident in the softening lines of her expression. The subtle disarmament of her skepticism was almost palpable as she took the seat across from him.

"Online dating feels like swimming against the current, doesn't it?" Tom began, his elbows resting casually on the table, fingers entwined around a cup that seemed more a talisman than a vessel for caffeine.

"More like being caught in a riptide," Sarah replied, the laugh-lines around her eyes betraying a humor that belied her earlier unease. "Every profile is a wave that looks promising until you're suddenly flipped upside down and unsure which way is up."

"Ah, yes," he nodded, the shared struggle igniting a camaraderie between them. "And then there's the challenge of explaining to your kid why you're all dressed up just to sit in front of a computer screen."

"Exactly." She leaned forward, hands wrapping around her own coffee mug as if to draw strength from its warmth. "You want to believe there's someone out there who understands the late-night fevers and last-minute school projects, not just the candlelit dinners."

"Someone who gets that sometimes, 'Netflix and chill' actually means passing out on the couch to the soothing sounds of cartoons because you've been playing superhero all day," Tom added, the corners of his mouth lifting in an amiable grin.

"Or supervillain, depending on the day," Sarah quipped, the resonance of their mutual experiences fostering an invisible thread that wove through the space between them.

"Indeed," Tom agreed, his laughter a low rumble that complemented the melodic undertones of the background music. "But amidst the chaos, we hold onto hope, don't we? For that connection that says, 'Yes, this is what it's all about.'"

"Hope," Sarah echoed, the syllable hanging between them like a sacred promise. "It's the compass that guides us through the storms. Without it, we're just... adrift."

As they conversed, the world beyond their table seemed to recede, leaving only the shared frustrations and aspirations of two single parents navigating the labyrinthine world of online dating—and, just perhaps, finding in each other a beacon to illuminate the path ahead.

Sarah watched the steam pirouette from her cup, a whimsical dance that mirrored the lightness burgeoning within her. Across the table, Tom's eyes crinkled with mirth as he launched into an anecdote about his latest online dating misadventure, involving a woman who had confidently claimed to be 'fluent in all dialects of toddler babble.'

"Turns out," Tom said with a theatrical sigh, "her proficiency was grossly overstated. My son's nonsensical rambling left her utterly bewildered. I suppose it's true what they say— toddlers are the ultimate codebreakers."

"Ah, yes," Sarah chimed in, the laughter spilling from her like notes from a well-tuned instrument, "the enigmatic linguists of our time. I'm convinced my daughter is secretly the curator of some ancient, mystical language."

Their laughter mingled, swirling around them like the comforting embrace of an old friend, eroding the veneer of trepidation that had initially coated the atmosphere. There, amidst the cacophony of clinking cups and murmured conversations, a camaraderie blossomed, rooted in the rich soil of shared trials and tribulations.

"Speaking of mysticism," Tom continued, the humor in his voice now interlaced with genuine curiosity, "how do you find your center in this whirlwind we call single parenthood? For me, it's those fleeting moments of stillness after bedtime stories, where the world stands still, and all is right—even if just for a heartbeat."

"Center?" Sarah pondered, her gaze drifting toward the window, where the outside world hustled by in blissful ignorance of the sanctuary they'd discovered here. "I guess it's in those small victories—you know, when you manage to concoct a meal that's both nutritious and doesn't get instantly labeled as 'yucky' by the harshest of critics."

"Ah, the culinary tightrope walks," Tom nodded sagaciously. "An art form unto itself."

Their conversation ebbed and flowed, delving deeper into the realms of their values, threading through discussions on the aspirations they held not only for themselves but for the young lives they were each shaping. It was in these exchanges that the tapestry of their kinship was woven—with every tale of parental trial, with every shared ideal of nurturing resilient and compassionate children, they found themselves more profoundly aligned.

"Ultimately, it's about providing a beacon for them, isn't it?" Sarah mused, her voice a reverent whisper that carried the weight of her conviction. "To illuminate the path ahead with love and wisdom so that they might navigate life's seas with an inner compass calibrated to kindness and integrity."

"Exactly," Tom affirmed, his expression one of earnest agreement. "If our legacy is to be measured, let it be by the happiness and heart we instill in our offspring."

In the sanctuary of the coffee shop, amidst the symphony of daily grind and caffeinated alchemy, Sarah and Tom discovered a resonance between them—a harmony composed not merely of laughter but of shared dreams and steadfast commitments. They were two souls charting similar courses through the unpredictable waters of life, finding solace in the reflection of their own hopes mirrored in the eyes of another.

Sarah's laughter faded into a soft smile as the topic gently shifted, like autumn leaves transitioning to winter's embrace. The frivolity of their banter retreated, giving way to a more tender dialogue, one that required the currency of trust and the courage of authenticity. Tom's gaze lingered on her, his eyes pools of understanding, as he recounted a particularly trying evening when his son's fever had spiked, and he felt the walls of his home close in with worry.

"Those are the moments," Tom's voice dipped, a timbre of solemnity threading through his words, "when you realize how solitary this path can be. How you're both the anchor and the sail in your child's life."

Sarah nodded, the motion a silent echo of empathy. Her fingers traced the rim of her coffee cup, an absent-minded gesture that belied the storm of emotions brewing within. "I remember a night like that," she began, her voice barely above the hum of the espresso machine's gentle purr. "It was just after the divorce—my daughter, she couldn't understand why bedtime stories were now a solo act. I held her as she cried for what felt like hours, feeling utterly alone in the ache of her longing."

In the shared confessions of their parental tribulations, there was an unspoken pact being forged—a mutual acknowledgment of the hardships that shaped their daily existence. It was in these raw admissions that the scaffolding of a deeper connection was constructed, each candid revelation serving as a testament to their resilience.

As if compelled by an invisible force, their hands found each other atop the reclaimed wood table, a simple touch that spoke volumes. Tom's thumb brushed against Sarah's palm in a silent solace, acknowledging the rough terrain they'd each navigated as solo guardians of young hearts. Her fingers responded with a gentle squeeze, affirming the sentiment.

Their eyes met, locking in a gaze that transcended the casual chaos of the coffee shop. In that prolonged look, there was an exchange of unvoiced promises and uncharted possibilities. The soft crinkles at the corners of Tom's eyes spoke of laughter weathered by time, yet undiminished in its capacity to bring joy.
Sarah's own eyes shimmered with a newfound light, reflecting an allure that was not merely physical but resonated from the depth of shared experience.

A smile whispered across Sarah's lips, one that was mirrored by Tom's own upturned mouth—a tacit admission of the pleasure found in this unexpected companionship. The intimacy of their interaction was subtle, yet palpable, an intangible wisp of connection that danced around them, hinting at the potential of a kindred journey yet to unfold.

Sitting there, with hands tentatively linked and souls bared in quiet confession, they were two voyagers momentarily anchored in a safe harbor, discovering the warmth of a bond that might, with time, guide them through the fog of solitude towards a horizon aglow with the promise of shared tomorrows.

Sarah, on the precipice of departure from the quaint cocoon of the coffee shop, paused to regard Tom with an expression awash in the soft glow of potential. Her heart, a once- guarded fortress, now felt the stirring of silken banners unfurling in the gentle winds of optimism. The conversation between them had meandered through the labyrinths of their individual lives, touching upon the tender walls erected by past tribulations, and yet here they stood, at the threshold of something that whispered of rejuvenation.

"Thank you for today, Tom," she said, her voice a melodic concoction blending gratitude with a tremulous eagerness to dive into the chapters yet written. "I haven't laughed like this in... well, I can hardly recall."

"Neither have I, Sarah," he replied, the timbre of his voice carrying the weight of sincerity,   as if each syllable were a stone laid upon the foundation of a nascent edifice of companionship. "Perhaps we should do this again? There's a world of anecdotes we've barely skimmed."

Her nod was a silent sonnet, rich with the lyricism of burgeoning curiosity. As Sarah turned to leave, an unwitting smile played upon her lips—a harbinger of the myriad possibilities that now seemed within reach. Each step away from Tom and the comforting embrace of the coffee shop felt less like retreat and more like the measured advance toward an alluring unknown.

Outside, the city breathed its relentless rhythm, and Sarah's phone, a sudden interloper in the symphony of her thoughts, vibrated with the urgency of the present. She glanced at the caller ID, her brows knitting together in a tapestry of perplexity—it was a number she did not recognize, yet one that tingled with the disquiet of familiarity. A breath held, a moment suspended, she answered.

"Hello?" Her inquiry floated into the void, met with silence that stretched, taut and expectant, before a voice from the other end shattered the stillness.

"Sarah Martin?" The question, stark and invasive, bore an undercurrent of significance that sent a ripple through the calm waters of her day.

She affirmed her identity, her grip tightening around the phone, the device suddenly transformed into a conduit for unforeseen tribulations. The line crackled with the static of hesitation before the voice, disembodied yet laden with an unspoken history, broke the tension.

"Sarah, it's about your past. We need to talk..."

The words hung in the air, a specter of conflict lurking at the edges of her newfound hope, threatening to eclipse the warmth of connection with the chill of shadows yet to be revealed. And as the chapter ended, it left behind a trail of questions, a breadcrumb path for the reader to follow into the forest of unfolding narrative.

Chapter 5

Sarah stepped into the bland beige room, her heels clicking sharply against the speckled vinyl flooring. She paused just beyond the doorway, scanning the lumpy circle of mismatched chairs and their nervous occupants. Some sat rigidly upright while others slouched low with arms crossed defensively, but all emanated a guarded vulnerability that Sarah knew all too well.

She chose an empty chair near a kind-eyed man who offered her a small smile. Before she could sit, he stood and extended his hand.

"You must be Sarah. I'm Tom, the group leader." His voice was gravelly yet gentle. "Let me introduce you to a few of our members."

Tom gestured to a slender woman with fiery red hair. "This is Rebecca. She's been with us for about a year now. Rebecca has a wealth of wisdom when it comes to navigating the online dating world."

Rebecca gave a little wave, her numerous bracelets jingling.

"And this is Michael." Tom indicated a bald, athletic man who sat straight as a rod. "He's one of our veterans here. Michael really understands the importance of thoroughly vetting potential partners before meeting them."

Michael nodded curtly at Sarah. She thought she detected a hint of sadness in his eyes.

"And finally, we have Emily." Tom motioned to a bubbly brunette who looked far younger than the rest of the group. "She just joined recently but has already brought such a bright spirit to our little family."

"Happy to be here!" Emily chirped with unbridled enthusiasm.

Sarah listened intently to each introduction, absorbing every detail. She felt a swell of anticipation, knowing she was surrounded by people who understood her unique struggles. For the first time in years, she didn't feel quite so alone.

Sarah took a seat in the circle of chairs, smoothing her skirt underneath her. She noticed the others leaning forward, their body language open and engaged.

Tom began, "Let's start by going around and sharing a bit about our personal stories with online dating. Feel free to talk about the highs and lows, the triumphs and tribulations."

Rebecca jumped right in. "Well, I signed up for one of those swipe apps after my divorce last year. I must admit, it felt empowering at first to be in control and choose who I wanted to talk to. But it got old real fast." She rolled her eyes. "Most of the guys just wanted hookups or didn't match their photos at all."

The group chuckled knowingly. Michael added in his baritone voice, "I hear you. I've tried all the apps over the years. Matches that seem promising at first, but then disappear or turn out to be married." He shook his head, a tinge of bitterness in his tone.

Emily piped up, "I don't let it get me down! Sure, I've had some horror stories, but I just laugh them off. Like the guy who brought his mom on our first date!" She snorted with laughter.

The mood lightened as the group swapped dating mishaps and commiserated over shared experiences. Sarah sensed the strong bond between them. It was her turn to share.

She took a deep breath. "I'm feeling really overwhelmed trying to date again as a single mom. I want to find love, but I have to protect my daughter first." Sarah recounted a recent coffee meetup that ended with the man propositioning her crudely. She shuddered at the memory.

"I never know who I can trust. But I don't want my bad experiences to make me close myself off entirely. It's a tough balance, and I could really use some guidance." She looked around hopefully, relieved to have opened.

Rebecca nodded understandingly. "It's so hard trying to date safely as a single mom. I've learned to watch for red flags from the start and trust my intuition."

She explained, "If a guy seems too eager to meet up right away, pushes for personal details too fast, or asks inappropriate questions about my child, I end it. Your safety is the priority."

Rebecca's voice softened with empathy. "And don't ignore those gut feelings even if you can't pinpoint why. If something feels off, it probably is."

Sarah listened intently, comforted by Rebecca's advice. It resonated with her own uneasiness lately.

Michael added, "I also recommend running basic background checks, especially once you move from messaging to actually meeting someone."

He continued, "Search online records, social media, anything you can find. Make sure their story checks out."

Looking at Sarah kindly, he said, "It's work, but so important to verify who someone really is before letting them into your life and your child's."

Sarah felt immensely grateful for their guidance. With their support and wisdom, she felt more empowered to navigate the dating world safely. She would proceed with greater caution and trust her instincts.

Emily smiled warmly at Sarah, her eyes twinkling. "Enough with the serious talk - don't forget to have fun too!"

She chuckled, tucking a curly lock behind her ear. "I once showed up for a first date and the guy looked nothing like his photo. I mean nothing. He was bald and had a huge beard!"

The group laughed as Emily continued, "Turns out it was his old college picture from like 10 years ago. We still had a nice chat over coffee but romantically it was a no-go."

She grinned. "You have to laugh at the absurdity sometimes. Don't take it all so seriously."

Sarah smiled back, immediately put at ease by Emily's lighthearted nature. She seemed so vibrant and full of life.

The conversation shifted as Tom said, "On a more serious note, it's so important to discuss boundaries and core values upfront once you start getting more serious with someone."

Rebecca nodded. "Being open about having a child is critical. Not everyone is equipped for that responsibility."

Michael added, "And don't be afraid to ask the hard questions about their past relationships, family issues, even finances. Better to know now if you're incompatible."

Sarah soaked up their guidance. Communication and transparency would be key in evaluating potential partners. She wanted someone deeply committed to her and her child.

The group spent the next hour sharing tips for having those difficult but necessary talks. Sarah left feeling empowered, with a new understanding of how to approach online dating as a single mom. She was grateful for the community she had found.

Sarah leaned forward in her chair, looking thoughtful. "I'm curious how you all approach introducing a new partner to your child once things start getting more serious. Any advice?"

The group members glanced at each other, nodding in acknowledgment that this was delicate territory.

Tom spoke up first. "For me, I've found it's important not to rush things. Take the time to really get to know someone before any introductions happen."

Rebecca concurred. "Absolutely. I made that mistake early on and it was so disruptive for my daughter when the relationship didn't work out."

Michael added, "I usually wait at least 6 months before initiating any contact between a new partner and my kids. You want to be sure it's heading towards something real before complicating it."

Emily offered a different view. "I tend to involve my son pretty early on. He's a good judge of character and I value his impression."

The group discussed the merits of both approaches, recognizing the need to balance protection of the child with openness.

Tom summed it up well: "There's no perfect answer. You have to listen to your intuition and know what feels right for your family."

The parents all voiced their agreement, realizing there were many gray areas when dating as a single parent. Patience and care for the child's wellbeing had to come first.

Sarah felt relieved hearing their perspectives. She wouldn't rush into anything but also stayed open to possibilities, knowing she had the group's support.

After a lull in the conversation, Tom suggested, "We should put together some guidelines or a checklist focused on online dating safety and communication. Could be helpful."

The group embraced the idea. Together they brainstormed ideas for vetting potential partners, having critical conversations, and evaluating compatibility as a single parent.

Sarah left the meeting feeling she had gained valuable new insights into navigating the dating world. This group would be an ongoing source of wisdom for her journey ahead.

Sarah took a deep breath as the meeting ended. She felt a swell of gratitude for the group's openness and support. Though they came from different social classes, she now counted them as friends.

"I can't thank you all enough for your advice today," she said. "It's such a relief knowing I'm not alone in this dating journey. You've given me renewed hope and determination."

Around her, heads nodded, and smiles grew.

"We're in this together," Michael said, placing a reassuring hand on her shoulder. "Don't hesitate to reach out, anytime."

Sarah blinked back tears, touched by their kindness. For the first time in a long while, she felt she was part of a community. A tribe who understood her struggles and uplifted her dreams.

Tom began passing out slips of paper for everyone to share their numbers. "Let's stay connected outside of meetings too," he said. "Maybe we can get together socially, offer support through text or calls."

There were murmurs of agreement as they exchanged details. The parents chatted casually, making plans for meetups at a cafe or park. The energy in the room was lighter now, filled with camaraderie.

When it was time to leave, Sarah gave hugs all around. They had come into her life when she needed them most. She would be forever grateful for this newfound family.

As Sarah stepped outside, she felt the cool evening air refresh her spirit. The future seemed bright with possibility. With the group behind her, she was ready to navigate the dating world with resilience and hope.

Sarah took a deep breath as she stepped outside, feeling the cool evening air refresh her spirit. The support group meeting had left her feeling empowered and inspired.

She reflected on all the valuable insights and advice the other members had shared. Rebecca's tips on spotting red flags, Michael's strategies for background checks, Emily's humorous dating mishap stories - it had all resonated with Sarah. For the first time in a while, she didn't feel alone in her struggles.

As she walked to her car, Sarah replayed the stories they had told, their openness and vulnerability. She knew she could trust these people, this newfound community. They would have her back through the difficulties of dating as a single parent.

Lost in thought, Sarah suddenly caught a glimpse of Tom as he exited the building behind her. He smiled warmly, his eyes crinkling in the corners. Taken aback, she smiled shyly in return.

In that moment, she felt a spark of connection to Tom she hadn't expected. There was something comforting yet exciting about his presence. Sarah wondered if there could be something more between them.

Shaking her head, she pushed the thought away. Tom was just a member of the group, there to provide support. Still, as she drove off into the night, Sarah couldn't ignore the lingering sense of possibility that now seemed open before her.

Sarah took a deep breath as she drove, the night air rushing in through the open windows. She was ready - ready to embrace whatever challenges and possibilities lay ahead in her journey of online dating.
The road stretched out endlessly into the darkness, but she no longer feared where it led. With the support and wisdom of her new community, Sarah knew she could navigate any treacherous

waters with resilience and hope.

She thought back to the stories the others had shared, tales of dishonest suitors, uncomfortable first dates, and ghosting. Sarah knew she would encounter similar obstacles, but the group had equipped her to handle them with grace. Their advice on trust, safety, and communication rang in her mind.

Glancing at her phone on the passenger seat, Sarah considered reactivating her dating profile. The very thought no longer filled her with dread. She felt strong enough to wade through an endless sea of matches and missteps to find someone worthy of her heart.

As a single mother, Sarah knew a potential partner would have to embrace both her and her child with open arms. She would not settle for less than full acceptance. With the group's support, she could take the time needed to find a true partner.

The road ahead would be long, but Sarah was ready for the journey. She drove on into the night, her heart filled with cautious optimism. The world was filled with possibilities, and she would boldly seek them out, one step at a time.

Chapter 6

Sarah Martin swept into the warm embrace of the coffee shop, the aroma of freshly ground beans intertwining with an undercurrent of anticipation that hovered in the air. She found her companions nestled in a secluded corner, where Rebecca Johnson sat, her red hair cascading like autumn leaves around a visage marked by the quiet resilience of motherhood. Beside her, Michael Turner's robust frame was folded into a chair that seemed too small for his athletic build, his graying temples lending him an air of distinguished experience. And then there was Emily Davis, whose laughter tumbled through the room in rich, sonorous waves, her animated gestures painting pictures of vivacity against the backdrop of mundane reality.

They were a triptych of hope and weariness, their stories woven from the same fabric of single parenthood, each thread colored with the contrasting hues of longing and trepidation. As Sarah joined them, the staccato of her heels on the wooden floor punctuating her arrival, she was enveloped by an atmosphere thick with camaraderie and a shared understanding that only those who have navigated the labyrinth of love and loss could truly comprehend.

As the conversation meandered through the trivialities and traumas of their collective experiences, Sarah listened with a meticulous ear, dissecting each narrative with the precision of a scholar unearthing ancient tomes. Her dark eyes, reflective pools of intelligence, widened perceptibly with every tale of digital courtship gone awry. The perils of online dating, once distant concerns whispered in the corridors of her mind, now clamored for attention with an urgency that was palpable.

Rebecca spoke of profiles that promised companionship but delivered solitude, her voice a delicate tremor that belied her stoic exterior. Michael recounted anecdotes tinged with a subtle humor that masked the gravity of encounters with individuals whose truths were buried beneath layers of deceit. And Emily, with her irrepressible optimism, nonetheless conveyed a hint of caution as she detailed the minefield that lay hidden behind charming avatars and flirtatious messages.

With each revelation, a mosaic of concern etched itself onto Sarah's features, the tableau of her face becoming a canvas upon which the chiaroscuro of online dating was painted in stark relief. It was not merely the stories themselves that fanned the flames of her apprehension, but the resonant chord they struck within her—a symphony of protective instincts that surged forth with maternal ferocity.

Here, in this alcove of introspection and espresso, Sarah's world was quietly tilting on its axis, the specter of vulnerability casting long shadows over her thoughts. Yet, amidst the burgeoning unease, a spark of determination kindled within her—a steadfast resolve to navigate these digital waters with the astuteness of one who has peered into the abyss and emerged undaunted.

Sarah leaned forward, her fingers tracing the rim of her coffee cup in a gesture that was both contemplative and decisive. She broke the companionable silence with a question that carried the weight of a mother's resolve. "What steps have you each taken to vet someone's authenticity online?" she inquired, her voice an intriguing blend of prudence laced with an almost childlike inquisitiveness.

Michael adjusted his glasses, a wry smile flickering across his face as he shared his tactic of reverse image searching profile pictures, a simple yet effective Sherlockian method to unmask the pretenders who lurk behind stolen identities. Rebecca chimed in with her own strategy, speaking of setting boundaries early on, her usual reticence dissolving into a stream of earnest advice about never sharing personal details prematurely.

Emily's chuckle was tinged with irony as she recounted her brush with a suitor whose criminal past unfolded before her through a happenstance Google search—a digital Pandora's Box that unleashed a tale replete with false aliases and unsavory records. Her laughter did not reach her eyes, which danced with a hint of triumph over the dodged bullet of potential peril.

"Have any of you encountered...let's call them 'digital doppelgangers'?" Sarah asked, her eyebrows arching with a mix of skepticism and genuine curiosity—the kind that comes from peering into the looking glass of another's experience hoping to catch a reflection of one's own fears and precautions.

The trio exchanged knowing looks, their collective experiences weaving a tapestry of cautionary tales. Michael spoke of a charismatic charmer, a veritable Casanova of the internet age, whose allure crumbled under the scrutiny of a background check revealing a litany of petty crimes. The atmosphere grew dense with tension, the previously light- hearted banter now replaced by the gravity of reality's intrusion.

"Fake profiles are just the tip of the iceberg," Rebecca added, her tone sobers despite the levity still playing at the corners of her mouth. "It's the skillful manipulators, those puppeteers of affection and trust, who truly pose the greatest threat."

Their stories unfurled like a scroll of digital misadventures, each anecdote a thread in the complex web of online dating—a web that Sarah now found herself entangled in, her mind churning with stratagems to shield her and her child from the potential hazards that seemed all too prevalent in this modern quest for companionship.

Sarah's questioning gaze shifted to Emily, who had remained conspicuously silent during the recounting of digital doppelgangers and criminal courtships. The subtle furrowing of her brow betrayed trepidation, and it was as though the coffee shop's ambient melodies had dimmed in anticipation of a sobering confession. "I... I fell for it," Emily's voice barely rose above a whisper, yet it resounded with the weight of shattered illusions.

The others leaned in, their expressions a tapestry of worry lines and empathetic shadows cast by the dim lighting. Sarah's heart clenched, a visceral response to the vulnerability that Emily exuded; it was a mirror reflecting her deepest anxieties about venturing into the labyrinthine world of online romance.

"His profile seemed impeccable," Emily continued, her hands wrapped around her cup as if seeking warmth from the recollection of a cold deception. Her initial excitement over meeting someone who was a kindred spirit—a fellow single parent with a penchant for literature and a genuine interest in her life—had been palpable.

"His messages were like sonnets, tailored to the very essence of what I believed love could be," she confessed, a hint of wistfulness threading through her cautionary tale. Yet, as she painted the portrait of her suitor, the charm that had once gleamed now tarnished by the cunning subterfuge beneath, it became apparent that the man she had envisioned was an artifice crafted by a maestro of emotional fraud.

"Then came the request for help—an emergency, he said." Emily's narrative culminated in the revelation of his plea for financial assistance, a meticulously woven fabrication designed to exploit her compassion and motherly instincts. The truth emerged as stark and cold as the untouched pastries on the table between them—the charming facade had masked a predator lurking in the digital reeds.

"By the time I realized what had happened, it wasn't just my finances that were drained," she sighed, the pain of betrayal etching deeper lines into her features. "It was my confidence... my trust."

As Emily's story unfolded, Sarah found her own resolve hardening amidst the tempest of emotions. It was a testament to the cunning that thrived in the shadows of virtual connections, preying on the unwary. And yet, here they sat, united by their misadventures, a fellowship tempered by adversity and a shared commitment to navigating the treacherous waters of online dating with eyes wide open and hearts cautiously guarded.

As the disquieting silence stretched between them like an ominous chasm, Sarah's heart thrummed with chilling recognition. Mirth had been the companion of their earlier exchanges, but now a palpable dread descended upon the cozy enclave of the coffee shop. Her gaze, once buoyant with the camaraderie of shared experiences, grew heavy-laden with the spectral shadows of trepidation that clung to Emily's confessional tapestry. The quagmire of online dating, once a labyrinth of potential romance, now revealed itself as a minefield strewn with duplicitous intent. Sarah felt the gravity of their vulnerability, her maternal instincts flaring like a beacon in the twilight of their shaken trust.

It was not merely the thought of monetary loss that etched fissures of fear into the bedrock of her composure; it was the harrowing contemplation of what might have transpired had the deception burrowed deeper into the fabric of their lives, entwining with the innocent threads of their children's existence. The specter of such peril loomed over her, a gorgon lurking amidst the digital missives and profile pictures, its gaze threatening to petrify the hope that had once animated her pursuit of companionship.

Yet, within the crucible of this newfound apprehension, Sarah's indomitable spirit began to forge a countermeasure to the malaise that threatened to engulf them. With a voice tempered by the alloy of caution and resolve, she broke the silence that had ensnared the group. "We can't let fear dictate our journeys," she intoned, her words casting ripples across the stillness. "But we're steering through uncharted waters, friends, and it's time we chart a course with eyes unclouded by the siren songs of false suitors."

Her suggestions unfurled like the tendrils of a protective spell, each one imbued with the wisdom of hindsight and the clarity of foresight. "Let's establish our own vetting rituals," she proposed, "a shared lexicon of red flags and safe harbors." She spoke of video calls as a bulwark against the chimeras of text-based personas, of background checks as the lighthouse guiding them away from the reefs of criminal histories, and of privacy measures that would serve as armor against the invasive inquiries of those with nefarious designs.

"Consider it our collective manifesto," Sarah declared, her countenance alight with the embers of determination, "a declaration of our right to seek happiness without falling prey to the wolves that roam the cyberspaces between us." Her suggestion was a clarion call, a rallying cry for vigilance that resonated with the protective instincts that safeguarded not only their hearts but the innocent souls that depended on them.

In that moment, Sarah's humor—a gallant defense against the bleakness—peered through the solemnity of her discourse. "After all," she quipped with a wry smile, "if Odysseus could navigate the perils of the Aegean, surely we can conquer the odyssey of online dating without being devoured by modern-day Cyclopes masquerading as Prince Charming."

Sarah's eyes flickered with the spark of an epiphany, a beacon cutting through the fog of uncertainty that had shrouded their table. "What if," she began, her voice steady as the thrum of anticipation grew within her chest, "we carved out our own corner in this digital labyrinth—a sanctuary for those of us threading the delicate balance between parenthood and the pursuit of companionship?" The idea unfurled like a flag upon the pole of her resolve, signaling a new venture on the horizon.

"Imagine a platform," she continued, her words painting the air with strokes of innovation, "meticulously tailored for single parents. A place where the vetting is stringent, the intentions transparent, and the safety of our children paramount." Her proposal held the gravity of law and the grace of poetry, a testament to the duality of her spirit, both warrior and sage.

The faces around her, Rebecca's etched with the resilience of countless small victories, Michael's imbued with the stoic kindness of a seasoned heart, and Emily's aglow with the gentle strength of quiet endurance, all mirrored back the brilliance of Sarah's vision.

Their expressions morphed from the shared weariness of battle-scarred comrades to the bright visage of crusaders glimpsing the dawn of their redemption.

"Sarah, that's... it's brilliant," Rebecca breathed out, the weight of past tribulations lifting in the presence of possibility. Michael nodded, his usual reticence giving way to the warmth of approval, "A haven for us, by us—where we set the rules of engagement." And Emily, ever the empath, added softly, "To think of our children playing in the background while we forge connections without fear—it's the peace of mind we've yearned for."

Their voices coalesced into a chorus of affirmation, each note resonating with the timbre of gratitude and the pitch of hope. It was as if Sarah had reached into the wellspring of their collective yearnings and drawn forth the vessel that would carry them across the treacherous waters, they had each navigated alone.

In that cozy enclave, amidst the clinking of coffee cups and the murmur of other patrons lost in their own worlds, a pact was silently forged. They were pioneers on the precipice of the unknown, ready to leap into the void with the assurance that their linked arms could bear the weight of their aspirations. Together, they would sculpt reality from the clay of their convictions, shaping a future where the only shadows cast were those of lovers in the glow of newfound connection.

Sarah Martin's gaze swept across the intimate circle of trust she had come to cherish, the familiar faces of Rebecca, Michael, and Emily reflecting at her not just the shared history of heartaches and missteps in the digital quest for companionship, but now also the glimmer of collective strength. It was a subtle shift, like the soft click of puzzle pieces falling into place, their edges no longer jagged with isolation but smoothed by the realization that their solitary battles were, in fact, a shared crusade. Her mouth curved into a smile, wry and knowing, as the air thrummed with the electricity of camaraderie.

"Imagine," she mused aloud, "a tapestry woven from our individual threads, each story a vibrant hue, together creating a safety net that could catch any of us should we stumble along this path." The metaphor hung between them, a palpable vision of unity and protection.

Rebecca leaned forward, her laughter lines crinkling with earnest intent. "It's more than a net, Sarah—it's armor. An armor forged from our collective wisdom, shielding us from the deceptive arrows flung by faceless avatars."

Michael, who often cloaked his insights in silence, chimed in with uncharacteristic animation, "An arsenal, if you will, where our experiences become the very weapons, we wield against the specters of deceit lurking behind screens."

And Emily, her voice usually a gentle whisper, rose in agreement with a fervor that belied her delicate frame, "A fortress where our children can play in the courtyard while we, the vigilant sentinels, watch over the ramparts."

The weight of Sarah's previous trepidations seemed to dissolve into the heady brew of potential and purpose that filled the room. Here was a fellowship bound by the common thread of seeking meaningful connections amidst the digital chaos, a round table of hopeful hearts ready to rewrite the rules of courtship.

"Then let it be so," declared Sarah, her tone a masterful blend of levity and solemnity that only those who have stared down vulnerability could genuinely appreciate. "We'll forge this new realm with the steel of our resolve and the warmth of our mutual endeavor."

They nodded, a silent accord passing through their midst, as if their thoughts had coalesced into a single, unspoken vow. No longer would they navigate these waters as solitary vessels; they were now a fleet, sails billowing with the winds of change.

"Here's to our pact," Sarah said, raising an imaginary chalice, her eyes alight with the kindle of hope and the fierce glow of determination. "To a future where the search for love is not a gamble with the unknown, but a journey safeguarded by the vigilance of a tribe united."

"Here, here!" the group echoed, their voices harmonizing in a chorus of solidarity, as the coffee shop became an unwitting witness to the birth of a new vanguard. Their pledge was a testament to the power of shared purpose, a beacon to guide others traversing the untamed wilds of virtual romance.

And thus, the chapter closed, not with a full stop, but with an ellipsis leading to the promise of new beginnings—a band of warriors armed with empathy and insight, champions of a safer future for single parents in the ever-evolving realm of online dating.

Chapter 7

Sarah tapped her fingernails on the table, staring at the glowing screen of her laptop. Another message from a faceless profile, another crude advance from a stranger. She sighed and closed the lid, the sound echoing in the empty kitchen.

Enough was enough. The world of online dating had become a minefield for her as a single mother, full of liars and lechers hiding behind charming words and carefully curated photos. The dangers were real - she'd heard too many horror stories from other single moms to ignore. But she refused to give up on finding love again. Sarah was nothing if not determined, with the strong will to take control of her own destiny.

She stood, straightening her smart pencil skirt, and headed for the hallway closet with purposeful strides. Her heels clicked decisively on the hardwood as she retrieved a large whiteboard and easel. Soon colorful markers were squeaking across the board as Sarah mapped out her plan, scribbling words like "verification", "background checks", and "video profiles".

This wasn't just about her anymore, she realized, but all the single moms struggling through the murky waters of online dating. She would create a new platform, one that puts safety first by requiring identity confirmation and criminal checks. No more hiding behind smoke and mirrors - only real people looking for real relationships. And she would see it through, come hell or high water. Sarah capped the marker with a flourish, admiring her work. The seed was planted. Time to get building.

Sarah tucked a strand of dark hair behind her ear as she studied the whiteboard intently. Her notes and diagrams represented more than just an app idea - they were the first step to making the online dating world safer for single parents everywhere.

A knock at the door shook Sarah from her thoughts. She opened it to find Alicia, a single mom from her support group, waving a store-bought pie with a smile.

"Hey girl, brought something sweet to fuel all that planning!" Alicia said, stepping inside. Her warm brown eyes scanned the whiteboard notes with interest. "This is looking so good already. We're all behind you 100%."

Sarah felt a swell of gratitude for her fellow single moms. "Thanks, it means everything to have your support. I want to make sure I get this right."

She ushered Alicia to the sofa where they dove into an animated discussion about app features. The camaraderie between them was evident as they bonded over dating disasters and dreams of finding real romance despite the challenges of single parenthood. Sarah's vision was now their shared mission.

The chatter halted at another knock - this time a lanky guy with glasses stood at the door, laptop bag slung over one shoulder.

"Jason! Right on time," Sarah welcomed him in. She turned to Alicia, "This is my friend Jason, he's a total tech genius and has agreed to help build the app."

Jason gave an awkward little wave then adjusted his glasses. "I've been coding since middle school - apps, websites, you name it. When Sarah told me her idea, I knew I had to help." He set his laptop on the coffee table, ready to dive in.

Sarah put a hand on his shoulder. "Jason has always come through for me. With his skills and our support group's input, I just know we can create something life-changing here."

Alicia raised her mug of tea. "Here's to making online dating safer and better for single parents everywhere!"

Sarah grabbed a notepad and pen and settled onto the couch next to Jason. "Alright, let's start brainstorming what features and safety measures we want to include in this app," she said, clicking the pen open eagerly.

"Definitely need to have background checks on all users," Alicia piped up. The other women murmured in agreement.

"Great idea," said Sarah, jotting it down. "We could partner with a screening service to handle that."

Jason nodded, opening his laptop. "I can build an integration with a background check API. We'll scrub for any red flags."

The conversation flowed freely as they tossed out feature ideas. Verified profiles with photo and video confirmation to prevent catfishing. A robust blocking and reporting system for inappropriate behaviors. Custom matching based on detailed parent profiles. Secure in-app messaging with encryption.

Sarah's pen flew across the pages as she documented their brainstorm. She wanted to create the safest, most tailored app possible for single moms and dads.

"Of course, we have to make it user-friendly too," Jason reminded them. "Safety is key, but a convoluted app won't attract users."

"True," Sarah circled 'intuitive interface' on her notepad. "Finding the right balance will be key."

The support group members shared their own dating app frustrations and horror stories. Sarah listened intently, determined to learn from past mistakes. She would conduct meticulous research to understand the pitfalls and advantages of existing platforms. This app would improve upon the status quo.

As the sunlight faded, Sarah felt a renewed sense of purpose. With her supportive community and Jason's technical prowess, her vision would soon become reality. For once, she allowed herself to feel truly hopeful about what the future held.

Sarah sat at her desk, powered up her laptop, and cracked her knuckles. It was time to draft a comprehensive project plan to bring this app to life.

She methodically outlined every step, from market research to launch. Sarah created a 12- month timeline with key milestones - product design, coding sprints, quality assurance testing. She set SMART goals - increase user engagement 20% month-over-month, achieved a 4.5-star rating within 6 months.

Sarah meticulously detailed each phase, highlighting dependencies and risks. User research would inform design requirements. Development relied on finalized UI mockups. Rigorous testing was essential prior to launch.

She assigned owners for each task, playing to the team's strengths. Jason would oversee all technical build. Sarah would drive user research, marketing, and funding. The support group would provide ongoing focus group testing and feedback.

Sarah's orderly nature and laser focus shone through in the comprehensive plan. She left no stone unturned, considering every angle and contingency. Her methodical approach would ensure smooth execution from start to finish.

Satisfied, Sarah emailed the project plan to Jason for review. She was eager to dig into the technical details with him soon. Though daunting, Sarah was energized by the roadmap they would follow to create something groundbreaking. This app wouldn't just be a passion project, but a catalyst for real change.

Sarah and Jason dove into the technical details during an animated brainstorming session. They were both buzzing with excitement about bringing Sarah's vision to life.

"Let's keep the interface clean and intuitive," Sarah said. "I want single parents to feel comfortable navigating it, even if they're not tech-savvy."

Jason nodded, jotting notes. "Absolutely. We'll use a simple, minimalist design. Icons and menus will be self-explanatory."

"And all our safety features need to be front and center," Sarah added. She ticked them off on her fingers. "Background checks, video verification, secure messaging..."

"Right," said Jason. "We could put badges on profiles that have been verified, so users know who they're dealing with."

The two continued bouncing ideas back and forth, building on each other's thoughts. Sarah felt grateful to have such an adept partner in Jason. He was able to translate her vision into technical specifications.

After finalizing the interface design, they dove into testing. Jason built a basic prototype app and demoed the key features. He showed Sarah how users would upload profiles, message matches, and access safety tools.

Sarah tested every pathway and edge case she could think of. She had Jason walk her through the verification processes and encryption to ensure they were bulletproof. As they uncovered issues, Jason would add items to his bug tracker for fixing.

After hours of exhaustive testing, Sarah leaned back satisfied. "I think this will be incredibly intuitive and secure for parents once launched," she said.

"We're well on our way," Jason agreed. "With your eye for detail and my technical skills, we'll build something great."

Sarah smiled, fueled by their momentum. She knew with meticulous planning and rigorous execution; their app would help so many feel safer in the dating world. This was just the beginning.

Sarah's eyes shone with determination as she considered the next steps for bringing the dating app to fruition. While she and Jason had developed an intuitive, secure platform, work remained to make it accessible to single parents nationwide.

"We need to get the word out," Sarah declared. "I want to reach as many people as possible. This can't just be a niche app - it needs to have an impact."

Sarah drafted meticulous plans for marketing and promotion. She researched successful app launches and made lists of publications, influencers, and organizations to contact. Her background in PR would be invaluable for crafting pitches and narratives.

"We should look into getting some seed funding as well," Jason suggested. "That could help us scale up faster."

Sarah nodded. "I have some connections with venture capitalists and angel investors from my work. I'll start putting together a pitch deck."

Over the next weeks, Sarah fired on all cylinders. She leveraged her network to schedule meetings with potential backers. Drawing on her charisma, she pitched her vision of empowering single parents in the dating world. Several investors were moved by her passion and signed on.

With funding secured, Sarah got to work on marketing. She ran energetic social media campaigns and placed targeted ads. She pitched the app's story to parenting blogs and niche publications. Momentum built as people learned about the platform.

As launch day approached, Sarah could barely contain her excitement.

"All our hard work is about to pay off," she told Jason. "Just imagine all the connections that will happen, and the safety this will provide. It's going to change lives - I just know it!"

Jason smiled. "Couldn't have done it without you - this app exists because you dared to dream it."

Sarah's eyes shone with gratitude and anticipation. The launch was only the beginning. She would continue working tirelessly to bring security and hope to single parents across the country. Her resolve was unshakeable.

Chapter 8

Sarah burst into Jason's dimly lit apartment, eyes ablaze with fiery determination.

"Jason, I need you!" she exclaimed as she marched across the cluttered living room. "Your coding skills could change lives - the lives of single parents just trying to find love again."

Jason peered up from his laptop, pushing his black-framed glasses up the bridge of his nose. "Whoa there, turbo. You can't just barge in here making demands," he said, raising an eyebrow.

Sarah plopped down on the sofa beside him. "Hear me out. I want to create a dating app exclusively for single parents - something safer and more secure than what's out there."

Jason sighed, his shoulders slumping. "You know that's not my thing. Building a secure app is serious business with a lot of potential risks."

Clasping her hands under her chin, Sarah gazed at him imploringly. "But you're the only one I trust who has the skills to do this. Think of all the good we could do, giving single parents a way to connect without compromising their safety."

Jason hesitated; uncertainty etched on his boyish face.

Sarah pressed on passionately. "I know we can figure the tech stuff out together. And I'll handle the rest - marketing, funding, whatever it takes. But I can't do this without you."

She squeezed his arm, her dark eyes gleaming with conviction. "Come on, Jase. This could change everything for so many people. I believe in this. And I believe in you."

Jason held her earnest gaze for a moment before a grin crept across his face. "Well, when you put it like that, how can I say no?"

Sarah whooped and threw her arms around him. "Yes! Let's do this. Together we're going to make dating safer for single parents everywhere. I just know it!"

Jason chuckled, patting her back. "Alright, alright. But we've got our work cut out for us."

As they launched into an animated discussion of app features and planning, Jason felt a spark of inspiration taking hold. Sarah's passion was contagious. This crazy idea could actually make a difference.

Sarah's living room was soon buzzing with lively debate about the proposed dating app. She and Jason huddled around her laptop; notebooks spread open as they brainstormed features to prioritize safety for single parents.

"Definitely need rigorous background checks," Jason said. "Multi-step screening process - employment and identity verification, criminal history, sex offender registry..."
Sarah nodded, jotting his ideas down. "And video profiles, so people can actually see who they're talking to. No more fake pics or catfishing."

"Good call. We'll make sure it's a live video, not prerecorded."

They discussed other precautions like blocking by location and mandatory unblurring of profile photos. Sarah's protective instincts as a single mom were in overdrive as she imagined all the ways creeps could exploit the system. But with Jason's tech expertise, she felt confident they could outmaneuver the dangers.

After finalizing an initial outline, Sarah invited members of her single parents support group over to share their perspectives. She introduced Jason and explained their vision for an app tailored specifically for single parents seeking relationships online.

"We want your real-world experiences to guide development," she said earnestly. "You know better than anyone what safety measures would help you feel more secure navigating online dating."

The group welcomed the chance to collaborate. As they traded stories and suggestions, Sarah could see Jason's eyes light up, his coding brain whirring with ideas. She smiled, knowing that together they could make this work. The app felt closer than ever to becoming reality.

Sarah opened the floor to the support group members, inviting them to share their thoughts.

Tanya, a single mom of two young girls, spoke first. "I tried online dating after my divorce, but it was so scary not knowing who I was really talking to. I'd feel much safer if I could do live video chats before meeting someone."

Others chimed in with their own hesitations about online dating as a single parent. Michael, a dad of a teenage son, said he wished background checks were mandatory. "I go into protection mode when I think about my boy meeting any of these strangers from the internet."

Sarah jotted notes rapidly as they offered suggestions: verified work and education histories, character references, mandatory unblurring of profile photos. She noticed Jason's leg bouncing excitedly as his fingers twitched, no doubt envisioning the coding involved.

After the group shared their insights, Sarah opened the floor to start brainstorming safety features. Hands shot up quickly with ideas.

"What about some kind of panic button inside the app?" suggested Tanya. "In case you feel unsafe during a date, you could alert friends where you are."

Michael added, "Definitely needs to include blocking by location range. I don't want any weirdos able to contact me if they live too far away."

As they called out their ideas, Sarah watched Jason furiously typing notes on his laptop. His intelligent eyes were glowing with purpose, showing his eagerness to turn these ideas into real protective measures for single parents seeking love online. She knew that together; they could build something truly meaningful.

Sarah smiled as she watched the support group members eagerly share their suggestions. Their passion for this project was palpable, and their insights invaluable.

After the initial brainstorming session, Sarah said, "Thank you all for these fantastic ideas so far. I want to keep this collaboration going, so let's schedule regular check-ins to refine the features and protocols."

She pulled out her calendar. "How about meeting every Tuesday evening for a status update and discussion?"

The group nodded enthusiastically. Mark, a single dad, piped up, "That would be perfect. We can track the progress and give feedback."

"Excellent," said Sarah. "Jason and I will work on developing a prototype, and we'll use our Tuesday meetings to walk through it together. Please test the features as we add them and let us know of any concerns."

Jason added, "We really want to identify any vulnerabilities early, so we can address them. Don't hold back on the critiques."

Tanya chuckled. "Oh, don't worry, we'll keep you on your toes!" The group laughed.

Sarah smiled. She appreciated their candor and looked forward to collaborating. With their insights and Jason's technical skills, she was confident they could create an app that would finally help single parents feel secure in online dating. The road ahead would take hard work and perseverance, but with this team, it felt achievable.

Here is a continuation of the scene focusing on the plot points you specified:

A few weeks later, Sarah and Jason gathered the support group members for an update.

"We've made good progress," Sarah began. "Jason and I divided up the tasks based on our strengths. I'm focused on research into existing platforms - what works, what doesn't, and where we can differentiate. Jason is spearheading technical architecture and coding."

Jason jumped in. "I created a timeline with milestones, so we stay on track. We'll need your help soon with user testing and feedback."

Tanya raised her hand. "I'm happy to help with testing. I used to work in quality assurance."

Mark added, "And I can lend a hand with coding if you need it."

Sarah smiled. "Perfect, thank you! I'll send out task assignments this week. Please let me know if you have bandwidth for more."

She continued, "On my research front, I've analyzed several popular dating apps. Many have minimal safety features beyond a basic verification system. We can really stand out by incorporating rigorous background checks and identity confirmation."

Jason nodded. "I'm prioritizing those safety protocols in the code. They'll provide peace of mind for single parents."

The group murmured in agreement.

"This is shaping up nicely," Sarah said, feeling motivated by their progress. "Let's keep up the momentum!"

The team left the meeting with renewed enthusiasm, ready to continue working towards their goal of a safer dating app. Though challenges remained, Sarah was confident that with this supportive group, they would succeed.

The next day, Sarah and Jason met to collaborate on designing the app's user interface.

"Let's keep it simple and intuitive," Sarah said as they sketched out screen flows. "As single parents, we don't have time to figure out complicated apps."

Jason agreed. "Absolutely. It should be easy to navigate and find matches."

They decided on a clean layout with straightforward menus and options. Swiping and messaging functions mirrored popular apps while unique safety features like identity verification were prominently displayed.

"I think this hits the right balance of familiar and innovative," Sarah said, pleased with their progress.

Jason added some final changes. "We'll get feedback from the parent group before finalizing. But this is a great start."

A few days later, Sarah emailed an update to the support group members. It included screenshots of the proposed interface along with a summary of other development progress.

"Let us know your thoughts!" Sarah wrote. "We want to ensure the app meets your needs and expectations before moving forward."

Feedback started trickling in over the next few days. Most were positive, with only minor suggestions for tweaks and enhancements.

Tanya requested larger font sizes for improved readability. Mark noticed a minor functionality bug in the messaging feature. Sarah and Jason diligently compiled all the feedback and planned revisions.

"This is so helpful," Sarah told the group during their next call. "Keep the suggestions coming. You're truly shaping this into the ideal app for single parents."

She was glad they had established open communication channels. It would ensure the app's design continued reflecting the real-world experiences of its intended users.

Sarah and Jason worked tirelessly over the next few weeks, incorporating the support group's feedback, and refining the app's features. As the launch date grew closer, an infectious energy and optimism filled the air.

One evening, Sarah invited Jason over for dinner as a small celebration.

"I can't believe how far we've come," Sarah said as they clinked glasses. "When I first pitched this idea, I wasn't sure if it would ever become a reality. But here we are!"

Jason smiled. "It's really shaping up. All the late nights and long coding sessions are paying off."

"I know there's still a lot to do before launch, but we should be proud of what we've accomplished so far," Sarah replied.

They discussed potential marketing strategies to spread awareness of the app within single parent communities. Sarah hoped that positive word of mouth would also help drive adoption.

As the evening wound down, Sarah felt a renewed sense of purpose. This app could truly make an impact and provide a safer, more trustworthy option for single parents seeking connections.

Jason gathered his things to leave. "The launch will be here before we know it," he said. "Then the real work begins!"

Sarah nodded. "I can't wait to get it into the hands of single parents. I think we're going to help a lot of people."

She gave Jason a quick hug before he headed out the door. As Sarah cleaned up, she pictured single parents across the country chatting and meeting through their app. All the effort has been worthwhile, she thought. This is just the beginning.

Chapter 9

Sarah and Jason sat side by side at the cluttered desk, laptops open and papers strewn about haphazardly. Sarah took a long sip of coffee, the rising steam fogging her trendy cat eyeglasses.

"Background checks are crucial for this app," she said decisively. "We need to make sure we're providing users with accurate information about potential dates."

Jason nodded, his fingers dancing across the keyboard. "Totally agree. I've been researching third-party services and found a great one called SafeConnect that specializes in background checks." He turned his laptop to face Sarah. "Take a look - they've got a killer reputation and work with tons of dating sites already."

Sarah scanned the website, eyebrows raising with interest. "Impressive client list. And thorough screening too - criminal records, employment verification, the works." She smiled approvingly at Jason. "Nice find. This could be our perfect partner."

"That's what I thought too," Jason said, pleased she agreed with his choice. He was always eager to contribute, especially when helping a friend like Sarah find happiness again. "I can contact them this week to get the ball rolling on integration. We'll make sure to lock down user privacy and security too."

"Perfect." Sarah squeezed his arm warmly. "Let's do this." She knew that with Jason's technical skills, they could build background checks into the app seamlessly. This would provide an extra layer of protection that gave single parents like herself peace of mind. Her trust in Jason was implicit - she knew he always had her back.

Sarah picked up her phone and dialed the number for SafeConnect. As the call connected, she sat up straight, adopting her most professional tone.

"Hi, this is Sarah Martin from ParentMatch. I was hoping to speak with someone about integrating your background check services into our dating app."

The SafeConnect representative sounded friendly and eager to help. They discussed Sarah's vision for incorporating comprehensive background screening into ParentMatch, enabling users to make more informed decisions about potential dates.

The rep detailed the various checks SafeConnect could provide, from criminal records to employment verification to drug testing. Sarah asked thoughtful questions, making sure she fully understood their capabilities and limitations.

By the end of the call, they had hammered out a preliminary agreement. SafeConnect would connect their API to ParentMatch, allowing background check requests to be seamlessly submitted from within the app. Sarah and the project manager agreed to an initial timeline for integration.

After hanging up, Sarah leaned back in her chair, feeling a sense of accomplishment. This had been a productive first step.

Besides her, Jason was already hard at work on the technical side. "I'm building the API calls to SafeConnect now," he said, eyes glued to his screen. "This will allow us to securely pass user data for the checks."

His fingers tapped swiftly over the keys. Sarah marveled at how quickly his mind worked. In no time, he had established a safe passageway between the two systems.

"There, all set," Jason announced. He turned to Sarah with a grin. "The background checks are ready for lift off."

Sarah smiled back, amazed at her friend's talent. With Jason's technical genius and her business savvy, they were well on their way to launching the most secure dating app for single parents. This milestone was worth celebrating.

Sarah cracked her knuckles, ready to dive into the next phase. "Alright, time to put this new feature through its paces," she declared.

They created fictional user profiles, inventing criminal records of varying severity. Jason set up automated test runs, flooding the system with background check requests.

At first, a few hiccups occurred. One check came back incorrectly, while another took longer than expected. Jason swiftly diagnosed the issues, adjusting the API calls and tweaking the connection settings.

Within an hour, the tests were running smoothly. Background checks zoomed back and forth, delivering accurate results at lightning speed. Sarah and Jason high-fived, thrilled to see their hard work paying off.

"I think we're ready to open the floodgates," Jason said. "Time to switch over to live data."

Sarah agreed. They uploaded profiles from willing testers, initiating real background checks through SafeConnect's massive databases.

The results poured in, painting detailed pictures of the testers' histories. Sarah scrutinized each report, verifying their precision.

A minor bug appeared, causing a duplicate search under one profile. Jason quickly patched the bug. He optimized a few other facets, ensuring users received only the freshest, most reliable data.

By the day's end, the background check feature was finely tuned and ready for launch. Sarah's apprehension had vanished. This new tool would empower users with vital information, creating connections built on trust. She couldn't wait to see it in action.

"I'd say our work here is done," Jason said, satisfaction evident in his voice. He began packing up his laptop, ready to stop for the day.

Sarah nodded, pride swelling in her chest. Today marked real progress toward their goal of building a safer dating app. Thanks to diligent testing, users could dive in with confidence, knowing ParentMatch had their backs.

With the background check feature now smoothly integrated into the app, Sarah knew it was time to get feedback from real users. She reached out to the single parent support group she had collaborated with throughout the development process.

"Hi everyone," Sarah wrote in an email. "We're ready to begin testing the full app, including the new background check feature. I'd love for you all to create profiles and try it out. Your real-world insights will be invaluable as we fine-tune things before the official launch."

She emphasized the importance of thorough testing and asked the group to provide candid feedback on their experience. "Please let me know if you have any concerns or suggestions," Sarah added. "Your perspectives as single parents are so important."

The responses came flooding in. The support group was eager to participate. They understood the value of rigorous vetting in creating a safe dating environment.

Tina replied first: "Count me in for testing! I'll create a profile this weekend. So glad you're taking safety seriously."

David added: "Background checks seem like a smart move. I'm happy to test the feature and provide my thoughts."

One by one, the support group members pledged their help. They were invested in the app's success and wanted to ensure it met the needs of single parents like themselves.

Sarah smiled as the emails accumulated, feeling grateful for the group's enthusiasm. With their assistance, ParentMatch's background check feature would provide the level of security and trust needed to facilitate meaningful connections. She couldn't wait to hear their feedback.

Sarah and Jason scheduled a video call with the support group to walk them through the testing process.

When the call began, Sarah's face appeared on screen, her expression warm and welcoming. "Hi everyone. Thanks so much for agreeing to help us test the new background check feature."

Jason jumped in, his geeky enthusiasm shining through. "We've created temporary profiles for each of you in the app's testing environment. I'll send you the login info now." His fingers clacked over the keyboard.

"Once you're logged in, you'll see an option to initiate a background check under the settings menu," Sarah explained. "Just enter your personal details and click submit. The system will automatically cross-reference various public records databases to verify identity and check for any red flags."

"Things like criminal records, bankruptcy, active restraining orders - anything that could raise safety concerns," Jason added. "The results should populate within a few minutes."

Sarah nodded. "Take some time to run checks on your profiles and get familiar with the feature. Let us know if you have any trouble accessing or understanding the results."

"And please give us your honest feedback on the user experience," Jason said. "Even small tweaks can make a big difference."

The support group members nodded along, taking notes. Tina spoke up first. "I like that it's easy to find under settings. And fast results are good too."

Sarah smiled. "Great, we're looking forward to hearing everyone's perspectives. Your input is so valuable at this stage."

The call wrapped up with Sarah and Jason fielding a few technical questions. Then the support group members logged into their test profiles, ready to fully explore the new background check feature. Their participation represented a crucial step toward building a safer, more trustworthy platform for single parents seeking meaningful connections.

Sarah and Jason scheduled weekly video calls with the support group to discuss their feedback on the background check feature.

"Let's start with the positives," Sarah said, clicking her pen open. "What's working well so far?"

Tina jumped in first. "I like how easy it is to initiate a background check. Just a few clicks and you're good to go."

Others chimed in with nods of agreement.

"The results are really comprehensive too," added Mike. "It covers education, employment, criminal history - basically everything you'd want to verify."

Jason smiled, pleased to hear the feature was user-friendly and robust.

"Have you noticed any inaccuracies in the reports?" he asked. "We want to ensure the data is airtight."

The group shook their heads. "Seems accurate from what I can tell," said Lily.

Sarah made a note. Accuracy was critical.

"How about areas for improvement?" she asked. "Don't hold back!"

"Well, the mobile experience could be smoother," Mike said. "The desktop view is fine, but it's a little clunky on my phone."

Sarah nodded. Mobile optimization was important.

"And it would be nice to have some kind of summary graphic for the results," Tina added. "Just a simple visual indicator of pass or fail."

"Great suggestions," Jason said, typing furiously.

The meeting continued with members offering tweaks and reporting minor bugs. Sarah and Jason took diligent notes, probing for more details and insights.

After each call, they prioritized the feedback, patching bugs, enhancing features, and smoothing out rough edges. Within a few weeks, the background check was running far more smoothly thanks to the support group's keen observations.

Sarah and Jason conducted one final round of rigorous in-house testing. Poring over the reports with scrutinizing eyes, they verified that the data was complete, accurate and securely accessed.

"I think we've got a strong foundation here," Sarah said, reviewing the final batch.

"Yeah, this is ready for primetime," Jason agreed. "Our users are going to feel so much more secure."

They high fived, celebrating the major milestone. Then it was on to the next big task: video verification.

Sarah's eyes lit up as she considered the possibilities of video verification. It would add such an important layer of authenticity for their users. No more filtered photos or clever camera angles - singles could see each other clearly via live video chat.

"Video is so key for building trust," she said excitedly. "I love this idea!"

Jason nodded, his mind already churning through the technical considerations. High-definition streaming, intelligent fake-detection algorithms, intuitive interface controls - it was a complex undertaking.

"It's doable, but will take some work," he said, grabbing a notepad to jot down ideas. "We'll need to optimize streaming quality, security protocols..."

He trailed off, scribbling an extensive list. Sarah peered over his shoulder, chiming in with her own wish list of features. After a lengthy brainstorming session, they had sketched out a comprehensive blueprint.

Jason cracked his knuckles, eager to sink his teeth into the coding. He was in his element, architecting an innovative system from the ground up. Sarah knew that with his skills, they would make rapid progress.

"Let's check in again in a few days once you've got some prototypes ready," she said. "I want to be hands-on with this one and test it extensively."

Jason nodded, already absorbed in his computer screen. Lines of code began filling his monitor as he built the foundations of their video verification system. Sarah left him to it, confident that soon singles would forge connections safely through clear video chats.

Sarah returned a few days later to check on Jason's progress. He had been working tirelessly, fueled by coffee and his passion for coding.

"It's really coming together," he said excitedly, demoing the video chat interface on his screen. "I optimized for HD streaming and low latency using WebRTC. And built an AI to detect manipulated media."

He showed Sarah the backend machine learning algorithms that could spot fake or synthesized videos. She nodded approvingly.

"This looks fantastic," she said. "Have you tested it yet?"

Jason shook his head. "Wanted to run tests together. We should simulate real world use cases."

They spent the next several hours running trials. Jason sets up profiles with AI-generated profile photos and videos. Then he and Sarah took turns video chatting, while the AI attempted to catch the fakes.

After multiple tests, they analyzed the results. The system identified manipulated media with over 95% accuracy. But there were still some edge cases that slipped through.

"We should tweak the sensitivity thresholds here," Sarah pointed out, examining the metrics.

Jason agreed, adjusting the algorithms. They continued testing and iterating until both were satisfied with the video verification capabilities.

"I think we've got something solid here," Jason said finally. "Once we integrate with the app, we can get the support group to beta test it."

"Great idea," said Sarah. "Their feedback will be invaluable before launch."

They high-fived, proud of the secure video feature they had engineered together. It would go a long way toward building trust and safety, helping single parents find true connections.

Sarah and Jason scheduled a final meeting with the support group to demonstrate the new video verification feature. They gathered in Sarah's living room; laptops opened as Sarah and Jason prepared to walk them through it.

"We're really excited for you to try this out," Sarah began. "As you know, safety is our top priority for the app. Video verification is the next step in building trust between users."

She nodded to Jason, who launched into an explanation of how the algorithms could detect manipulated media and prevent catfishing. The support group listened intently, understanding the value of this extra layer of security.

"We'll need your help testing it to smooth out any last bugs," Jason concluded. "Your profiles are already loaded so you can video chat with each other and see it in action."

The support group eagerly began initiating video calls, chatting casually while the verification ran in the background. Sarah and Jason watched over their shoulders, making notes on any glitches that appeared. After an hour of thorough testing, the group provided their feedback.

"That was seamless," said one member named Lily. "I felt totally at ease, like I was just having a normal video call with a friend."

Others chimed in with positive impressions, reassuring Sarah, and Jason that the feature was ready for launch. They discussed a few minor tweaks to the interface to improve user experience, but overall were satisfied.

"This is going to make such a difference for single parents on the app," said a member named Caleb. "I feel like I can really trust who I'm talking to now."

Sarah smiled broadly. "That's exactly what we hoped to accomplish. Thank you all for your time and input - it's so valuable."

The support group left feeling enthused about the new video feature that would enable safer online dating. Sarah and Jason celebrated the successful final test, their app one step closer to changing their lives.

Sarah and Jason walked the members of the support group to the door, exchanging hugs and handshakes. After they had left, Sarah let out an exhilarated laugh.

"We did it!" she exclaimed, turning to Jason with a brilliant smile. "The video verification is ready to go live."

"We make a great team," Jason replied, grinning as he gave her a high five. "All that testing and tweaking really paid off."

Sarah nodded. "I know there's still work to be done before launch, but I feel like we've climbed a mountain here. Video verification was such a complex feature to implement, and we pulled it off."

"Couldn't have done it without your leadership and vision," said Jason. He started tidying up the papers scattered around the desk.

Sarah leaned back in her chair, reflecting on their journey so far. It hadn't always been easy, but each milestone achieved brought them closer to their goal. She felt a deep sense of purpose, knowing this app would empower single parents seeking love.

"I can't wait to see the look on the beta testers' faces when we give them access," she mused. "This is going to change online dating for them."

"It's pretty incredible that our app can make the world a little safer," Jason said. "We should be proud of what we've accomplished together."

Sarah nodded; her eyes gleaming with anticipation. "The launch will be here before we know it. Then the real work begins as we grow the user base and refine things."

"One step at a time," Jason said. "For now, let's celebrate this big achievement."

Sarah smiled, her heart swelling with hope and excitement. The future looked bright for their app and its mission to revolutionize online dating for single parents.

Chapter 10

Emily strode into the church basement, her curly brown hair bouncing with each energetic step. A vibrant smile lit up her face as her gaze swept over the familiar circle of chairs filled with other single parents. She was ready to dive into this week's support group meeting.

The fluorescent lights hummed softly overhead as a dozen tired but determined eyes turned to welcome the new arrival. Though the room's faded avocado walls and scratchy blue carpeting had seen better decades, the space radiated a warmth and kinship forged through shared struggles.

Emily settled into the empty seat between Janelle, a softly smiling mother of three, and Hank, a perpetually exhausted yet quick-witted father of twins.

"Rough morning wrangling the munchkins, Hank?" Emily teased.

Hank sighed dramatically, though his eyes glinted with humor. "Let's just say the double stroller has earned its retirement."

Janelle leaned over with a knowing nod. "I remember those days. It does get easier."

Emily smiled, feeling a rush of gratitude for this little community. She couldn't imagine navigating single parenthood without their empathy, wisdom, and - when needed - comic relief.

For the next hour, joys, trials, and tips were shared. Emily chuckled along with Janelle about potty training mishaps, then offered Hank an extra container of homemade mac and cheese.

As the meeting ended, Emily realized just how much she cherished this space, this sanctuary from the loneliness and judgment that often-accompanied single parenting. She hoped she could offer the same support to those who came after her.

With a contented sigh, she gathered her things and headed for the door, re-energized for the week ahead.

Emily paused at the doorway, turning back to face the group with an impish grin.

"Before I go, I have a little announcement."

All eyes turned to Emily as she practically bounced on her toes, barely contained excitement radiating from her smile.

"I've been secretly dating someone I met on Hinge!"

Emily's admission burst forth in an infectious laugh, her eyes dancing with joyful mischief. She clasped her hands, awaiting the group's reaction.

A ripple of surprise moved through the room. Hank's eyebrows shot up. Janelle tilted her head, lips pursed in concern. Whispers were exchanged as they processed this unexpected news.

"Hinge? But I thought we'd all agreed to stick with Single Parents Meet?" Hank scratched his beard, confusion furrowing his brow.

Janelle nodded, leaning forward. "Emily, honey, are you sure that's safe? We talked about the risks of those more mainstream apps."

Emily's smile faltered slightly as she read the worry etched on their faces. She knew they only wanted to protect her and her daughter. But she was tired of living in fear, of denying herself companionship.

"I know, but I was hoping...maybe this time it would be different." Emily bit her lip. She wanted them to understand, even if they didn't fully agree. "I just want a chance at happiness. We all do, right?"

Janelle and Hank exchanged uncertain glances. The room filled with murmuring as the group wrestled with empathy and caution, support, and concern.

Emily stood rooted in the doorway, vulnerability creeping into her hopeful expression. She needed their guidance, but even more, their trust.

After a heavy silence, Hank leaned forward, compassion softening his features. "Why don't you come back and tell us about this fella. We've got your back, kiddo."

Relief washed over Emily as she rejoined her circle, the people who understood her hopes and fears more than anyone. This conversation was far from over, but she knew they would figure it out together.

Emily made her way back to her seat, her smile returning as she felt the support of the group surrounding her.

But as she sat down, Janelle leaned in, her eyes narrowing. "Emily, I have to ask. Did you meet this man on Tinder?"

Emily's face fell. She nodded hesitantly.

"Oh Emily..." Janelle sighed, shaking her head as she crossed her arms. The rest of the group shifted uncomfortably.

"We talked about this," Hank said gently. "Those big dating sites just aren't safe for single parents. Too many creeps looking for easy targets."

"I know, I know," Emily said, dropping her gaze. "But I was so careful. We video chatted a few times first, and he seemed totally normal."

Janelle furrowed her brow. "Honey, that's what they all seem like at first. But you can't know someone's true colors until you meet them in person."

The group murmured in agreement. Emily felt their care and

concern like a heavy weight.

"Please, just be smart about this," Hank said. "For your sake and your little girl's."

Emily nodded, tears pricking her eyes. She knew they only wanted to protect her. But she was so tired of living in fear, of denying herself a chance at love.

There were no easy answers. But surrounded by people who understood that struggle, Emily felt hopeful they could find a way through together.

Emily took a deep breath as she looked around the room at the concerned faces of her support group.

"I know you're all just trying to look out for me," she began. "And I really appreciate that. But..."

She trailed off, gathering her thoughts. Hank leaned forward, his kind eyes encouraging her to continue.

"But I don't want to live my life in constant fear," Emily went on, her voice growing stronger. "I want to be open to love, even if that means taking some risks."

Janelle started to interject, but Emily held up a hand.

"Let me finish," she said gently. Janelle nodded, sitting back in her chair.

"I met Brian on a dating app, yes. And I know that comes with dangers. But we video chatted for weeks before meeting up. I did my research, checked his social media. He seems like a genuinely good guy."

Emily looked around the room again, making eye contact with each person.

"You've all taught me so much about protecting myself and my daughter. And I swear, her safety is still my top priority. But I owe it to both of us to be open to finding a partner, someone who could become family."

She smiled softly. "I really think Brian could be that person. I just ask that you trust me to handle this responsibly. And support me as I take this chance."

The group was silent for a moment as her words sunk in. Then Hank reached out and squeezed her hand.

"You're right, Emily," he said. "I'm sorry if we came on too strong. We just want you to be happy."

Murmurs of agreement circled the room. Emily exhaled, relief washing over her. She knew the road ahead wouldn't be easy. But with this group behind her, she finally felt ready to walk it.

Emily nodded gratefully at Hank. She appreciated the support but knew there was still more to discuss.

"I understand your concerns," she said, addressing the group again. "As parents, we have to worry about every possibility. But sometimes, that worry can hold us back from living fully."

She paused, gathering her thoughts. "After my divorce, it was so hard to imagine ever trusting someone again. The dating world felt dangerous, like one misstep could ruin everything. But I was lonely. And I owed it to my daughter to model healthy relationships."

Emily made eye contact with Janelle, who had been the most vocal with her doubts.

"Janelle, you mentioned how hard it's been, raising the kids alone after losing your husband. I can't imagine that pain." Janelle looked down as Emily continued. "But you deserve to find love again when you're ready. We all do."

The group nodded, a wave of understanding passing between them. They'd each sacrificed so much for their children. It was time to prioritize their own happiness.

Emily smiled, feeling the mood shift. "So, let's support each other. Share ideas, look out for red flags. But also, be open to the magic that could be waiting for us online."

She squeezed Hank's hand, then addressed the group one last time. "We can do this. We can find love safely. I know it."

Chapter 11

Sarah Martin sat hunched over her sleek laptop, the soft glow of the screen reflecting a tapestry of anticipation in her eyes. She was on the precipice of launching an app designed with the diligence of an expert craftsman, tailored to stitch together the fragmented world of single parenting with the silken threads of solidarity and support. As the digital clock on her desktop ticked away, aligning itself with the appointed hour, she initiated the launch sequence with the precision of a maestro conducting a symphony's crescendo.

The virtual space, once a void, now brimmed with the burgeoning presence of her creation. Sarah observed, as though through a microscope, the first tentative steps of users navigating the labyrinth of her app's interface. Their avatars, glowing orbs of potential connections, traversed the platform with cautious optimism, much like single parents would meander through the playgrounds of new relationships.

As the user count climbed like ivy up the walls of indifference that had long surrounded the single parent community, Sarah couldn't help but let a triumphant smile dance across her lips. Yet, her elation was not without the company of vigilance; for she knew too well the delicate balance between innovation and responsibility, having woven into the app's fabric an array of safety measures, each a sentinel standing guard over the vulnerability of its users.

However, with popularity spreading its wings like a social butterfly, feedback began fluttering in, carrying with it the weight of concerns over the app's strict safety protocols. Sarah received the messages with the stoicism of a seasoned general reading reports from the frontlines. The users, those brave souls seeking connection amidst the chaos of solo child-rearing, found themselves at odds with the fortress of security checks that stood between them and the promise of companionship.

Each expressed concern chipped away at the monolith of Sarah's confidence, yet she remained resolute, her belief in the necessity of these measures as unwavering as a lighthouse amidst tempestuous seas. For Sarah, who had navigated the treacherous waters of trust after her divorce with the tenacity of an ancient mariner, understood that the safe harbor provided by stringent safety protocols was not just a feature but the very keel keeping the ship afloat in the stormy world of online dating.

Thus, the scene sets the stage for a conundrum most profound: the reconciliation of safety with freedom, the harmonization of protection with possibility—a symphony Sarah was determined to compose with both the passion of a romantic and the prudence of a sentinel.

Sarah hunched over her laptop, fingers poised like a concert pianist ready to unleash a sonata upon the keys, as she initiated the virtual town hall—a digital agora where discourse would flow as freely as the pixelated streams of video feeds. Her screen brimmed with the mosaic countenances of single parents, each a portrait of concern within their own domestic galleries—a tableau vivant of trepidation against the backdrop of Sarah's safety edicts.

"Good evening," Sarah intoned, her voice a melodic blend of authority and empathy, resonating through the speakers and into the homes of her audience. "I understand there are concerns regarding our app's safety measures, and I am here, as open as a book whose pages yearn for annotation, to discuss and address your thoughts."

The forum erupted, not chaotically, but with the fervor of pent-up frustrations seeking an outlet, as messages cascaded down the chat panel like a waterfall of collective apprehension. One user, her avatar a defiant phoenix rising from the ashes, articulated the prevailing sentiment with succinct eloquence: "We appreciate protection, but we're not porcelain dolls locked in a cabinet. We need space to breathe, to connect without feeling shackled by overzealous safeguards."

Sarah listened, her mind a sponge absorbing the droplets of discontent, nodding with a practiced gravitas that belied the cogs turning tirelessly behind her observant gaze. She formulated her response with the meticulous care of an alchemist transmuting base metals into gold, her words chosen to reassure yet assert the primacy of security in this brave new world they were all navigating.

"Freedom," she began, her tone a blend of Socratic dialogue and maternal assurance, "is not the absence of constraints but the presence of safeguards that allow us to soar without fear of Icarian falls. Our protocols aren't chains but lifelines, ensuring that when you reach out across the void, there is something solid to grasp onto."

The contention swelled, as though Sarah had struck a chord that resounded with dissonant harmonies throughout the digital congregation. A father, his profile picture a lone oak standing sentinel in a field, fired back, his message infused with the passion of a debate champion on the cusp of delivering a coup de grace. "Lifelines can become nooses if wound too tightly. We seek love, not lockdowns. Trust must be both given and received."

Sarah felt the weight of his words, heavy as an anchor dragging along the seabed of her convictions. Yet, she stood firm, her rebuttal a fortress constructed with the stones of experience and the mortar of necessity. Her reply was a tapestry weaving together the threads of her own journey—of trust shattered and slowly, painstakingly reconstructed.

"Trust," she replied, her voice steady as the keel of a ship cutting through stormy seas, "is the most precious commodity in the currency of human connection. But it is not a blind leap into the abyss; it is a calculated stride taken with eyes wide open. The foundation of our platform is built on that very principle—to provide a space where trust can flourish, tempered by the wisdom of vigilance."

The debate continued, an intricate dance of opposing wills, each step a measure of conviction, every turn a display of commitment to their shared cause—the pursuit of connection in a world fraught with invisible perils. As the night drew on, the tenor of the conversation remained unresolved, a symphony reaching its crescendo without conclusion, leaving participants suspended in a state of animated stasis, the next movement yet to be composed.

Sarah, with a perspicacity sharpened by maternal instinct and the tribulations of her own narrative, surveyed the proliferating notifications on her smartphone—a modern Pandora's box unleashing a barrage of opinions and objections about her freshly launched app. Each ping heralded another voice clamoring to be heard, a user questioning the rigor of the safety protocols she had so meticulously crafted. Yet, in the maelstrom of discontent that swirled around her, Sarah remained an obelisk of resolve; her conviction in the sanctity of safeguarding single parents and their offspring was unassailable.

She understood, as only someone who had navigated the labyrinthine complexities of love and loss could, that the mantle of protection she offered through her app was not merely a feature but a pledge—a solemn vow to those walking the tightrope between hope and caution. It was this unyielding adherence to the tenet of security that furnished her with the fortitude to counter the backlash, her discourse seasoned with the wit that often accompanies those who dance along the precipice of innovation and tradition.

"An ounce of prevention is worth a pound of cure," she typed, her fingers deftly striking the keys with the rhythmic assurance of a maestro conducting an invisible orchestra. Her message, directed at the heart of the community she sought to serve, was an eloquent defense of the decision to encase the tender shots of new relationships within a carapace of digital vigilance.

"Dear fellow voyagers in the odyssey of single parenthood," she began, tapping into the wellspring of shared experience that united them, "it is our prerogative—nay, our duty—to arm ourselves against the potential storms that may arise from ill-considered liaisons. The features you decry are not shackles meant to constrain but rather lifelines cast into the turbulent seas of online dating to ensure that, should the waters grow treacherous, we are not swept away by the currents of deceit."

With a flourish, she dispatched her missive into the ether, a beacon of guidance for those navigating the shadowy realms of seeking connection in the digital age. Despite the cacophony of discordant voices, Sarah continued her crusade, extolling the virtues of the app's features with the fervor of a zealot, her rhetoric imbued with the levity that belies profound seriousness—championing the gospel of precaution with an unwavering smile that dared the world to challenge her ethos.

Sarah convened the digital assembly of her support group, a coterie of fellow single parents whose virtual companionship had become an anchor in her tumultuous seas. As she presented her screen's glowing tableau to the faces that flickered like candles against the encroaching dark of criticism, her voice—a sonorous blend of determination and warmth.
—carried through the pixels, gathering strength from the shared resolve that bridged their disparate locations.

"Esteemed allies," she declared, her tone weaving gravitas with the subtlest hint of whimsy, "we stand at the precipice of a great divide, with the winds of dissent buffeting the ramparts of our creation. Your counsel, in this hour, is the bulwark against which the tide of opposition shall break."

Nods and murmurs of solidarity emanated from the gallery, each participant a mosaic tile in the tapestry of encouragement that swaddled Sarah. Their words, though mere whispers traversing the circuits and cables, were as potent as a clarion call, rallying behind the flag that Sarah bore aloft—the standard of safety in the quest for affection and understanding.

Yet, even amidst this bastion of support, the tempest outside raged on. The forums and message boards, once havens of harmonious exchange, now crackled with the electricity of confrontation. Disgruntled voices, armed with the artillery of anonymity, launched volleys of invectiveness, challenging the ramparts of regulation that Sarah had so meticulously constructed.

"Your fortress of caution," one detractor thundered across the digital expanse, "is but a prison that stifles the very love it purports to protect!"

"Ah, but dear critic," Sarah parried with a deft touch of irony, "is it not better to navigate the labyrinth with a thread of Ariadne than to be devoured by the Minotaur of misfortune?"

The exchanges grew fervent, the staccato of clashing opinions reverberating through the virtual space as if echoing within the hallowed halls of debate. Sarah, ever the stalwart guardian of her principles, met each challenge with the poise of a seasoned diplomat, her ripostes tinged with jest yet cutting to the quick of the argument.

"Are we to discard our shields and gambol into battle unarmored?" she challenged, her query hanging in the air like a sword of Damocles above the heads of her opponents.

It was a dance as intricate as it was volatile, a pas de deux of ideologies locked in a fierce embrace. Each point and counterpoint, a step in this choreography of contention, drew lines in the sand that neither party seemed willing to cross. And as the crescendo built, the atmosphere thick with the heady perfume of heated discourse, Sarah remained the unwavering axis around which the maelstrom spun, her conviction a beacon that pierced the fog of disagreement.

In the crucible of conflict, where passions flared and tempers threatened to boil over into the realm of irrevocable words, the tenor of the struggle shifted. It was no longer a mere exchange of views but a testament to the enduring human desire to forge connections, even when such efforts are fraught with peril. And Sarah, with the chorus of her supporters rising behind her, faced the onslaught with the grace of a queen who knows her reign is just.

Sarah perched on the edge of her ergonomic chair, a fortress of screens in front of her—a general surveying the battlefield of public opinion. The cursor blinked impatiently on the document titled "App Improvement Strategy" as she chewed the end of her pen, contemplating the Gordian knot that lay before her. It was a delicate equation, balancing user satisfaction with the non-negotiable tenets of safety, each variable begging for her attention like sirens luring sailors to their doom.

With an exhale that carried the weight of her predicament, Sarah began typing, her fingers dancing across the keys with the precision of a pianist during an adagio movement. The list she compiled was a testament to her unyielding desire to harmonize the cacophony of concerns without losing the melody of security that underpinned her creation. She posited the introduction of a tiered verification system, which would afford users the liberty to choose their level of disclosure while still upholding a bastion of trustworthiness.

Next, she mused over the suggestion box feature—a digital olive branch to those who felt unheard. This virtual forum would not only collect feedback but also provide a transparent avenue for discourse and community-driven enhancements. She envisioned it as a council of sorts, where ideas could be debated and tested in the crucible of collective experience.

Her monitor glowed with the soft light of impending solutions, each paragraph a steppingstone towards an accord that might quell the unrest without sacrificing the sanctity of her digital haven. Sarah leaned back, allowing herself a wry smile, for in this labyrinth of compromise and innovation, she had found a thread to guide her through. It was a path fraught with uncertainty, indeed; yet she walked it with the swagger of a gambler who plays for keeps, knowing full well that the house might not always win, but neither does it fold without a fight.

Sarah Martin, the once-besieged architect of a digital fortress for single parents, now stood at the precipice of a defining juncture, her cursor a quivering arbiter between conciliation and the steadfast tenets she had woven into the very fabric of her creation. The murmurs of disgruntlement from a faction of her users, those who chafed against the stringent safety protocols that were the app's bulwark, swelled to a crescendo, besieging her inbox with missives that oscillated between plaintive dissatisfaction and outright indignation.

Her dark eyes, reflecting the tumultuous sea of contention that flickered across her screen, were unyielding flints sparking with resolve. It was in this critical, charged tableau that Sarah's mettle would be tested—would she capitulate to the clamorous demand for laxity, or would she remain an immovable sentinel guarding the sanctuaries of hearts seeking solace in companionship?

In the maelstrom of discordant voices, Sarah's mind coursed through channels of reasoning and retrospection, every synapse firing with the memory of past trials, the acrid tang of betrayal that once besmirched her trust, lending gravity to her conviction in these ramparts she had raised to shield others from similar fates. With the poised grace of a seasoned rhetorician, she drafted her response—a missive imbued with the gravitas of her experience, spiced with the subtle humor of one who has danced on the knife-edge of vulnerability, yet emerged with the fortitude of spirit intact.

"Dear Concerned Users," she began, each keystroke a note in the symphony of her unwavering stance, "our collective journey is paved with the desire for connection, a path we tread with the caution born of lives etched by the indelible ink of responsibility to those we hold dear." Her words unfurled on the digital parchment before her, an eloquent defense of the battlements she refused to dismantle. "The safety measures are not mere walls; they are the considered contours of a terrain designed to foster trust, ensuring that the footsteps we venture forth with are grounded in security."

It was a gambit of sorts, a high-wire act balancing the twin exigencies of user autonomy and uncompromised safeguarding of the vulnerable. Yet as she dispatched her epistle into the ether, there was no tremor in her hand, no falter in her heart. For Sarah Martin, enshrined within the algorithmic tapestry of her app, was the immutable belief that the sanctity of safety must never bow to the caprices of convenience.

The die was cast, and as the digital echo of her decision reverberated through the community, Sarah remained anchored in the certainty that her convictions were not just the bedrock of her enterprise but the compass by which she navigated the tempestuous waters of human connection. She would not yield, for in her estimation, the value of a single parent's peace of mind far outweighed the transient satisfaction of a disgruntled few seeking shortcuts through the labyrinth she had so meticulously charted.

Sarah toggled through the barrage of notifications; each a digital arrow aimed at the bulwark of her principles. The screen glowed like a tempestuous sea of discontent, the pixels awash with the fervor of those challenging her steadfastness. With each swipe, her resolve was tested; the cacophonous symphony of dissent challenging the orchestra of her convictions.

"Compromise," they demanded with unyielding insistence, yet she was no Pyrrhus to countenance such a hollow victory. The very fabric of her creation, woven from threads of meticulous care and unwavering vigilance, could not endure even the slightest unraveling without coming apart at the seams.

As the evening waned and the glow of her laptop cast long shadows across her determined visage, Sarah's fingers danced with a lithe grace upon the keys, crafting responses with both the precision of a surgeon and the eloquence of a poet. Her replies were parries and thrusts in an intellectual fencing match, where the stakes were as high as the safeguarding of hearts seeking solace in companionship.

Yet for every argument artfully dismantled, for every detractor assuaged, a new challenger rose to take their place in the digital arena. It was a Sisyphean endeavor, her task to reassure and educate unending, a hydra of concerns rearing new heads with each one addressed.

The moon had traversed its celestial arc when Sarah leaned back in her chair, eyes tracing the constellations of interaction on her screen as if searching the night sky for answers. The humor in the situation was not lost on her; she, a modern-day Cassandra, prophesying the perils that lurked within the cybersphere's deceptive embrace, while others clamored for the gates to be flung wide open.

But laughter found no berth in the gravity of her predicament. Unresolved conflict hung thick in the air, a miasma of contention and consternation that clung to her skin like the evening's humidity. It was clear that the morrow would bring no respite, no armistice in this silent war of words and ideals.

With the chapter closing, Sarah's silhouette against the dimming luminescence of her screen was a testament to her fortitude. The readers would lay their heads upon pillows that night, their minds abuzz with anticipation. They would wonder how this digital-age hero, armed with naught but her conviction and the keystrokes of her creed, would navigate the labyrinthine path ahead. Would she emerge triumphant, or would the tide of opposition erode the foundations of her digital sanctuary?

The cursor blinked expectantly, awaiting the next command, as the world held its breath for the unfolding saga of Sarah Martin's crusade in defense of the sanctum she vowed to protect.

Chapter 12

The candlelight flickered across Bill's chiseled features as he gazed at Sarah from across the intimate table. She tucked a strand of dark hair behind her ear, meeting his piercing blue eyes with her own hazel ones.

"So, tell me more about your work with the children's hospital. That's really admirable," Sarah said, taking a sip of her wine.

Bill smiled wryly. "Well, I can't take all the credit. It's rewarding to try and make a difference in those kids' lives, but I'm no saint."

Sarah detected a glimmer of something in his expression, a shadow that crossed his face before he hid it away again beneath an easy grin. What secrets do you hold? she wondered.

"We all have our pasts," Sarah offered gently. "What matters is what we do now."

Bill nodded, looking thoughtful. "Wise words. And very true."

They continued chatting animatedly, drawn together by their sharp wit and openness. Sarah marveled at how Bill understood her in a way no one had before. He read her, speaking to her unvoiced dreams and pains. It frightened and exhilarated her.

When the check came, Bill reached for it. "Please, allow me," he insisted with a roguish smile.

Sarah acquiesced, a thrill running through her. Here was a man who saw her, who didn't shy away from her strength. As they walked out into the night, she felt hopeful. The future suddenly seemed full of possibility.

Sarah gazed out the cabin window, taking in the sweeping

mountain vista before her. The snow-capped peaks gleamed in the morning sunlight, tranquil and enduring. She breathed deeply, filling her lungs with the crisp, pine-scented air.

"Quite a view, isn't it?"

She turned to see Bill emerging from the bedroom, his hair endearingly rumpled from sleep. He came up behind her, slipping his arms around her waist. She leaned back into him, comforted by his warmth and solid strength.

"It's beautiful here. So peaceful." She turned in his arms to face him. "Thank you for bringing me."

He brushed a strand of hair from her face, his expression tender. "I wanted to share this place with you. It's special to me."

They stayed like that for a moment, content in each other's arms as the sun continued its steady climb overhead.

Later, as Sarah chopped vegetables for an omelet, Bill sat nearby sipping his coffee, his eyes drifting over the newspaper headlines. She studied him discreetly, taking in the sharp line of his jaw, the way his forehead creased in concentration. He seemed so self-assured, so steady and wise. Yet she sensed a restlessness in him, subtle signs that he was not all that he appeared.

What secrets do you hold? The question echoed again in her mind. She longed to unravel the mystery of this intriguing, complicated man. But she knew she must be patient, go slowly.
The cabin filled with the warm scents of breakfast cooking. Outside, a crow's raucous caw broke the silence. Sarah smiled to herself, feeling somehow that she was standing on the edge of something new, a threshold she was ready to cross. The future shimmered before her, rich with promise.

Sarah's eyes drifted over to Bill's open suitcase on the floor near the bed. It wouldn't hurt to take a quick peek, would it? Just a tiny invasion of privacy to satisfy her growing curiosity about this man.

Setting down her knife, Sarah walked quietly over to the suitcase. Her heart pounded as she carefully lifted the lid.

It seemed perfectly ordinary - shirts, pants, toiletries. But her searching fingers found a hidden compartment along the edge. It clicked open, revealing a stack of IDs with Bill's photo but different names. Shocked, Sarah stumbled back.

"What is this?" She whirled around to see Bill standing in the doorway, his eyes hard.

"I can explain-" he began, but Sarah cut him off.

"Who are you really? Why do you have these fake IDs?" Her voice shook with emotion. This kind man she had trusted now seemed like a stranger.

Bill sighed, running a hand through his hair. "It's complicated, Sarah. I never meant to deceive you, but there are things in my past..." He trailed off evasively.

Sarah's shock was giving way to anger. "I think I deserve the truth. No more lies, Bill. Tell me who you really are!"

His shoulders slumped in defeat. "Alright. But you may want to sit down - it's quite a long story."

Sarah crossed her arms, standing firm. The cabin was silent except for the ticking of a clock on the wall. Finally, Bill began to speak, his words shattering the idyllic weekend getaway.

Bill took a deep breath and met Sarah's stern gaze.

"Those documents...they're just for my protection. I know it seems suspicious, but I have very legitimate reasons for needing them."

He paused, as if carefully considering his next words. Sarah said nothing, her posture rigid as she waited for him to continue.

"I used to work in a very dangerous field, Sarah. Powerful people wanted me dead. I had no choice but to assume new identities to stay safe."

Sarah's expression softened slightly at this, but her eyes remained wary.

"Why didn't you tell me any of this before?" she asked. "What exactly was this 'dangerous field'?"

Bill shook his head. "I wanted to, believe me. But it was too risky. I had to be sure I could trust you first."

He moved closer, his voice pleading. "I know it seems strange, but you have to believe I would never intentionally deceive you. My past is behind me now. You're the only thing that matters."

Sarah felt torn. She wanted to trust the man she had fallen for, but her instincts were screaming not to accept his story so easily. She needed answers.

"I'm sorry, Bill. But I can't just take your word for this. I need to know more about who you really are and what you've been involved in. I'm going to do some investigating of my own."

Bill's face paled at this, but Sarah's mind was made up. She had to know the truth, no matter what it revealed or who got hurt in the process. Her own safety, and that of her child, had to come first.

Sarah steeled herself as she dialed the number for the private investigator. She had agonized over this decision, but it was time to find out if the man she was falling for was truly who he claimed to be.

The PI picked up on the first ring. "Ms. Martin, I've been expecting your call. My preliminary search turned up some...concerning information about Mr. Simmons' background."

Sarah's heart sank, though she was not entirely surprised. "Go on."

"There's a long string of aliases, for starters. William Simmons is just the latest. I also found police reports of domestic disturbances at several of his prior residences."

The PI paused before continuing. "It appears your gentleman friend has a history of manipulative and abusive behavior towards past romantic partners. He somehow managed to circumvent the standard background checks on your dating app."

Shock and rage boiled up inside of Sarah. She thought of the evenings spent laughing with Bill, the future she had imagined they might share. It had all been a carefully crafted lie.

"I see," was all she could manage in response.

"I'll continue gathering evidence and send over a full report. For now, my strong recommendation would be to end things immediately for your safety."

Sarah thanked the investigator profusely before hanging up. Her sadness quickly turned to anger. She would not let Bill get away with deceiving and using her. It was time for a confrontation.

Grabbing her purse and keys, Sarah stormed out the door to her car. The drive to Bill's place was a blur. She rehearsed what she would say, imagining the look on his face when his web of lies finally unraveled.

This ended now. Sarah was ready to face the truth.

Sarah arrived at Bill's apartment building and marched up to his door, pounding loudly.

"Open up, Bill! We need to talk, now!" she shouted.

The door swung open, and there stood Bill, wearing a surprised expression.

"Sarah? What's going on?"

She stormed past him into the apartment. Wheeling around, Sarah confronted him directly.

"I know about the fake IDs, the police reports, all of it. Did you really think you could keep up this charade forever?"

Bill's face fell. He opened his mouth, but no words came out at first. Finally, he stammered, "I don't know what you mean, I..."

Sarah cut him off. "Don't play dumb. I had you investigated and found out about your history of abuse and deception. It's over, Bill."

Defeated, Bill slumped down on the couch and buried his head in his hands. When he looked back up at Sarah, his eyes were pleading.

"Okay, yes, I have a past I'm not proud of. But that's not who I am anymore, Sarah. Being with you has changed me. I know I should have been honest from the start, but I didn't want to lose you."

Sarah shook her head, unswayed. "How can I ever trust you now? My first priority has to be protecting myself and my daughter, not chasing some fantasy with you."

Bill stood and approached Sarah, but she recoiled from him.

"Please, Sarah, just give me another chance. I know we have something special, something worth fighting for. I'll do whatever it takes to regain your trust."

Taking a deep breath, Sarah steeled herself. As much as it pained her, she knew what she had to do.

"I'm sorry, Bill. I just can't take that risk. I think it's best if we don't see each other anymore."

And with that, she turned and walked out the door, holding back tears. She had loved the idea of Bill, but not the real man standing before her. It was time to move on, for her own good and for her daughter's.

Sarah left Bill's apartment with a heavy heart, but she knew ending things was the right decision. As difficult as it was, she had to prioritize protecting herself and her daughter over her feelings for Bill.

Once home, Sarah picked up the phone and called the police. She recounted the fake IDs she had found in Bill's suitcase and explained her suspicions about his motives for using the dating app. The officer on the other end assured her they would investigate it and thanked her for the information.

Next, Sarah logged into the dating app and left a review on Bill's profile, warning other users about what she had discovered. She tried to stick to just the facts, without letting her emotions get the better of her.

"Found fake IDs and documents among his belongings," she wrote. "Get the sense he is not who he claims to be. Proceed with caution."

It pained her to potentially ruin Bill's chances at finding love, but she knew she couldn't stay silent. Other single mothers deserved to know the truth.

After hitting send on the review, Sarah closed her laptop and let out a long sigh. She was saddened by how things had turned out, but proud of herself for having the courage to walk away when she realized Bill wasn't who she thought he was.

The next morning, after dropping her daughter off at school, Sarah arrived at the office, ready to dive back into her work on the dating app. This painful experience had only strengthened her resolve to make it a safe and supportive community for single parents.

She immediately got to work strengthening the identity verification process, determined to prevent another Bill from slipping through the cracks...Sarah sat at her desk, staring blankly at her computer screen as she reflected on the whirlwind romance and dramatic ending with Bill. She had really thought he was different-charming, attentive, and seeming to genuinely care about her in a way she hadn't experienced since her divorce. But it had all been an elaborate act to manipulate her, putting both her and her daughter in danger.

She shook her head, angry at herself for letting her guard down and ignoring the warning signs. The fake IDs should have been the final straw, but she had let herself get swept up in fantasy. Never again, she told herself. From now on, she would trust her instincts. If something seemed too good to be true, it was.

This experience had reinforced how careful she needed to be when meeting men online. As a single mom, her daughter had to be her first priority. She couldn't risk bringing unstable men into her life. It was better to be alone than with the wrong person.

Sarah vowed to herself that she would never again ignore red flags or rationalize away questionable behavior. She would listen to that inner voice telling her something was off. And she would walk away at the first sign of dishonesty - no matter how strong the emotional connection.

Her mission was bigger than her own search for love. She was determined to build an app where no other single mother would have to go through what she did. A place rooted in trust, safety, and community.

Sarah took a deep breath and turned her focus back to her computer screen. She began making a list of new security features to implement. This painful chapter was behind her, but her journey was just beginning.

Chapter 13

Sarah's fingers flew over the keyboard with a ferocity that belied the stillness of her surroundings. In the hushed confines of her home office, the only sound was the quiet tap- tap of keystrokes as she navigated the labyrinthine corridors of the digital world, her screen a flickering beacon in the dim twilight of early evening. She was on a quest, an unwavering champion of truth in the modern-day tournament of love and deceit, armed with nothing but her wits and an unshakable resolve to peel back the layers of obfuscation shrouding Bill's past.

Each click was a deliberate stride into the unknown, each opened tab a new chapter in the unwritten annals of William "Bill" Simmons' history. Sarah mined social media archives, scrutinized public records, and tapped into the less savory repositories of personal information that lay hidden in the murky recesses of the internet like sunken treasure. Her mind, an ever-whirring engine of deduction and analysis, processed the fragments of data with the precision of a virtuoso composer orchestrating a symphony of facts.

As she delved deeper into the electronic morass, a picture began to emerge—a mosaic of incidents and testimonies that, when viewed in isolation, appeared innocuous enough. But Sarah, with her discerning eye, saw the insidious patterns that began to form, a tapestry of manipulation woven from the threads of Bill's interactions with women who had once found themselves ensnared by his charms.

With each revelation, Sarah felt the walls of her reality tremble, her belief in her own judgment quaking as the evidence mounted. It was as though she were an archaeologist uncovering an ancient civilization, not of grandeur and enlightenment, but of malice and control. The shock that gripped her was visceral, a maelstrom of disbelief churning in the pit of her stomach as she unearthed court filings that spoke of restraining orders, whispered confessions on forgotten message boards, and a string of aliases that left her head reeling.

Her heart pounded a staccato rhythm against her ribcage, the growing trepidation like a shadow stretching across her conscience. Sarah's intellect wrestled with the implications, her humor—usually a wellspring of light in the darkness—now tinged with a sardonic edge as she imagined herself a protagonist in some tragicomic play, the unwitting fool in blind pursuit of a phantom prince charming.

The sense of unease that crept up her spine was not unlike the sensation one feels when standing at the precipice of a great height, the instinctive knowledge that a single misstep could send you hurtling into the abyss. Each new piece of evidence was a pebble dislodged underfoot, a harbinger of potential peril, yet onward she pressed, driven by a duty that transcended her own emotional turmoil—a duty to the truth and to those who remained oblivious to the danger lurking behind Bill's piercing blue eyes.

Sarah's fingers paused above the keyboard, suspended as though in a tableau of hesitation. The glow of the computer screen cast an otherworldly pallor upon her face—a silent witness to the internal cataclysm that waged war behind her eyes. Her mind became a battlefield where armies of anger marched against battalions of betrayal, clashing over the terrain of her fractured trust. How could she, Sarah Martin—a woman of perspicacity honed by the trials of single motherhood and professional ambition—have been so thoroughly deceived?

The revelation of Bill's past misconduct unfurled within her like some grotesque blossom, its petals saturated with the poison of his duplicity. An ireful heat rushed to her cheeks, a crimson tide of indignation at the thought of those piercing blue eyes—a hue she had once deemed oceanic and profound—now revealed as frigid pools wherein duplicity swam like some abyssal creature. Fear too made its serpentine presence known, whispering sibilant scenarios of jeopardy not just for her own well-being, but for the unsuspecting souls who traversed the digital corridors of the app, seeking connection, not predation.

The app itself, an edifice built on the promise of safety and camaraderie for those navigating the solitary waters of single parenthood, now threatened to become a trojan horse through which Bill might usher in his malevolent intent. The very fabric of its reputation quivered precariously on the fulcrum of this moment; Sarah knew that to allow such a man to operate within their midst was tantamount to leaving the gates unguarded, inviting calamity to befall those she had endeavored to shield.

A surge of responsibility flooded her veins, propelling her beyond the paralysis of her earlier dismay. Inaction was a luxury she could ill afford; the stakes were elevated, transcending the personal vendetta that simmered within her. The integrity of the platform was imperiled, the sanctity of its purpose now a vessel vulnerable to the insidious bilge of Bill's machinations. It dawned upon her with crystalline clarity: to remain passive was to permit further victimization by his practiced guile, to stand idly by while innocence was ensnared by his charade of charm.

"Action," she whispered to the silent room, a solitary vow that reverberated through the confines of her resolve. With renewed determination, her fingers danced once more across the keys, each tap a clarion call to fortify the digital ramparts and safeguard the community that had placed their trust in her hands. The jest of fate had played its hand, and Sarah Martin would not be found wanting in the act.

Sarah's cursor hovered over the 'compose' button, an unassuming rectangle that now felt as portentous as the trigger of a firearm. The weight of decision pressed upon her with an intensity that constricted her very breath; to confront Bill directly was an act not devoid of peril—her safety, a diaphanous veil at best against the potential onslaught of his reaction. Yet, to cower in the shadows, accumulating evidence while time marched inexorably onward, presented a different breed of danger—the insidious threat to those whose blissful ignorance she could shatter with but a few keystrokes.

She sat back in her chair, the leather creaking under the shift of her
resolve, thoughts tangling like a nest of serpents each vying for
supremacy. There was humor, dark and bitter, in contemplating
one's own jeopardy from a man she had once thought could be the
harbinger of new beginnings. Sarah could almost laugh at the
irony if it were not so mordantly laced with the potential cost of
human frailty.

"Patience," she muttered, the word slicing through the fog of her
indecision. It was a gambit to bide her time, a stratagem born of
necessity rather than inclination. With this silent pledge, she
turned her attention once more to the screen, delving into the
labyrinthine realms of social media and public records—a digital
archaeologist seeking the relics of Bill's concealed past.

Reaching out to mutual acquaintances required a deft touch, a
subtle inquiry here, an innocuous question there. Sarah cultivated
each interaction with the meticulous care of a chess master, each
move calculated to reveal without alarming, to inquire without
accusation. Her inbox slowly filled with responses that ranged
from the laconic to the loquacious, each a puzzle piece she
meticulously fit into the emerging mosaic of deceit.

"Ah, the plot thickens," she noted dryly as a particularly
enlightening email blinked into existence, its contents a
confirmation of suspicions rather than revelations. It was from
someone who had brushed the periphery of Bill's life, unwittingly
witnessing the rehearsal of a well-worn play whose script Sarah
was beginning to know by heart.

Each tidbit of information, each shared experience was a filament
she wove into a growing tapestry of formal accusation, the pattern
complex yet unmistakably damning in its intricacy. Her fingers
danced across the keyboard with a grace that belied the gravity of
their task, each keystroke a note in the symphony of her
investigation. She archived emails, cross- referenced dates,
triangulated testimonies—all with the precision of a maestro

conducting an orchestra of intel.

The portrait of Bill that emerged was one etched in the stark hues of control and manipulation—a canvas upon which he had painted himself as the protagonist in a tragedy of his own design. Sarah could feel the crescendo building within her, a fortissimo of truth that would soon need an audience. But not yet—not until every note was in place, every rest accounted for.

"Preparation is the companion of prudence," she murmured to the walls, the aphorism a buoy to her spirit amidst the tempest of data. Sarah Martin was no stranger to adversity; it had been an unwelcome guest at her table more times than she cared to count. Yet, as she pondered the penumbra stretching between the known and the unknown, between action and patience, she found a wellspring of humor in the role of reluctant detective—a role she had neither auditioned for nor desired but would play with all the aplomb at her disposal.

Sarah's sanctuary, the quiet nook where her computer hummed softly, had morphed into a command center. The glow of the screen cast a ghostly pallor on her determined face as she assimilated the fragments of Bill's past—each more perturbing than the last. Her heart hammered a staccato rhythm against her ribs, an echo of the urgency that seeped into her veins like ink in water. Here was an enigma, a man she thought she knew, unfurling into a scroll of warning signs and whispered rumors, all painting a picture of a predator masquerading in sheep's clothing.

"Time," she whispered, "is a luxury I no longer possess." Each click bore witness to a history tainted with emotional larceny, pulling Sarah deeper into a labyrinth from which emerging unscathed seemed a feat Herculean in nature. Bill's past relationships began to resemble archaeological strata; layers upon layers of subterfuge and coercion, with Sarah excavating the bones of truths long buried.

She parsed through records with an analytical eye, weaving the tenebrous threads of evidence into a tapestry of twisted affections.

It was imperative now, more than ever, that this clandestine architecture of duplicity be laid bare. Every email, text message, and anecdotal confession became a tessera in the mosaic of manipulation that was Bill's modus operandi.

"Only fools rush in where angels fear to tread," she mused, yet found herself sprinting headlong into the fray, armed with resilience and a burgeoning dossier of deceit. The hours waned, bleeding into one another until time itself seemed an abstract concept, irrelevant to the gravity of her purpose.

With meticulous precision, Sarah began to construct a timeline on a large whiteboard that dominated one wall of her study—a chronology of transgressions against the unsuspecting. Dates, names, and incidents were pinpointed with forensic accuracy, each a constellation in the dark firmament of Bill's machinations. Red strings crisscrossed like scars, connecting disparate events into a coherent narrative of predatory behavior.

"Pattern is the father of detection," she proclaimed softly to the room, a semblance of levity threading through her voice despite the somber task at hand. Her intellect engaged in a chess match with the specter of Bill's past, plotting moves and countermoves, anticipating feints within feints.

The final piece slotted into place—a testimony that mirrored those before it, yet singular in its incrimination. There it was, the irrefutable sequence of Bill's ill intentions strewn across her wall, a silent yet screaming indictment. Sarah stepped back, surveying the work with a mixture of pride and dread.

"Checkmate," she declared to the absent adversary, a wry smile gracing her lips. The game was far from over, but the battle lines were drawn, and Sarah Martin was not one to shrink from confrontation when the stakes were life's own currency.

Sarah perched on the edge of the ergonomic chair, her fingers hovering over the keyboard in a momentary stasis as the gravity of her next step loomed like an obelisk in her mind's landscape. The cursor blinked expectantly, a digital heartbeat syncing with her own accelerated pulse. To involve the authorities or not—that was the Gordian knot tightening around her conscience, each strand woven from threads of civic duty and self-preservation.

On one hand, she considered the Sisyphean task of single-handedly dismantling the edifice of Bill's deceit—an undertaking fraught with peril and uncertainty. Her thoughts cavorted with hypotheticals, a menagerie of potential confrontations that could escalate beyond her control. On the other, there was the labyrinthine bureaucracy of law enforcement, where her earnest crusade might become ensnared in red tape or dismissed by those jaded by one too many false alarms.

Yet, as she oscillated between action and inaction, a crescendo of responsibility swelled within her, a clarion call that could not be muffled by trepidation. It was the reckoning of risk versus rectitude; the scales tipped, inexorably, toward the latter. In the interstice between indecision and resolve, Sarah found clarity—a crystalline understanding that to marshal the forces of justice was the most sagacious path forward. After all, what is the purpose of society's guardians if not to shield the vulnerable from the wiles of wolves in sheep's clothing?

With a fortifying inhale that drew courage from the very ether, Sarah initiated the electronic summoning of the constabulary. She crafted an email with the meticulousness of an alchemist transmuting base metals into gold, each word imbued with evidence and urgency. Attachments accrued like appendages—screenshots, testimonials, the intricate web of her whiteboard investigation—transformed into a digital dossier of indictment.

"Dear Sergeant Lyle," she began, invoking the name of the local precinct's head of investigations, "I'm reaching out to present information regarding a matter of pressing concern..."

Her exposition was both eloquent and economical, threading the needle between alarm and articulation. She conjured the specter of

Bill's misdeeds without hyperbole, allowing the stark reality of the timeline to speak its thousand words with the brevity of a haiku.

"Whilst I am cognizant of the myriad demands on your department's resources," she typed, her keystrokes a staccato accompaniment to the metronome of her resolve, "I implore you to examine the attached evidence with due diligence."

Submission of the communique was the crossing of a Rubicon, the point of no return etched in binary code. As the digital missive winged its way through cyberspace, Sarah felt the mantle of whistleblower settle upon her shoulders—an amalgam of Joan of Arc and Deep Throat, sans armor or parking garage.

What followed was a telephonic exchange that danced the pas de deux of disclosure and discretion. Sarah's voice—calm yet underscored by the steel of conviction—narrated the saga of subterfuge that had unfolded behind the innocuous façade of Bill Simmons. Detective Lyle, his tone a blend of skepticism and intrigue, probed with questions honed sharply by years of parsing truths from lies.

"Rest assured, Ms. Martin," he intoned with the gravitas of one who understood the weight of such matters, "we'll look into it."

"Thank you," Sarah replied, the phrase a simple coda to the complex symphony of her endeavors. She replaced the receiver, her fingerprint a temporary relic upon its surface, and allowed herself the luxury of a measured exhale. The die was cast, the baton passed, the first domino nudged in a sequence that would lead, she hoped, to justice served with the blind impartiality of Themis herself.

The moment the folder, swollen with its compendium of damning evidence, slipped from Sarah's fingers and into the waiting hands of the authorities, a seismic shift reverberated through her. This tangible transfer of responsibility, akin to the mythic burden of Atlas shrugged, was accompanied by an effervescent surge of relief that bubbled up from the depths of her being. As if shedding an exoskeleton of dread, she felt lighter, liberated from the oppressive weight of secrets that were not hers to keep but too perilous to ignore.

In this act, Sarah Martin, whose existence had hitherto oscillated between the binaries of single motherhood and professional juggernaut, transmuted into the unlikely champion of those ensnared in Bill Simmons' web of deceit. Each shred of paper, every byte of data culled from the shadowed corners of his past now lay bare before the scrutiny of justice's unblinking eye—a tapestry of truth woven by her own steadfast resolve.

Emboldened by the certitude that she had marshaled all the resources at her disposal, Sarah stood as a paragon of vigilance. She had deftly navigated the labyrinthine channels of information gathering, donned the armor of due diligence, and emerged as the bearer of revelations most sinister. It was a role she had never auditioned for but one she had embraced with the stoicism of a seasoned sentinel.

As she stepped outside the precinct, the crisp air greeted her like the first breath after a plunge into icy waters. The sun, hanging low on the horizon, bathed her in aureate light—a silent ovation for the day's valorous deeds. Her thoughts meandered to the potential repercussions, the maelstrom of outcomes that could ensue from the unmasking of Bill's chicanery. Yet, even as the specter of retaliation loomed, she remained undaunted; the conviction that the moral arc of her actions bent toward righteousness was her bulwark against the tide of uncertainty.

The road ahead brimmed with the unknown, each step a foray into uncharted territory where the only compass was her own moral fortitude. She pondered the malleable nature of human connection, how trust once fractured could metamorphose into a prism through which the true colors of character were revealed. As dusk edged its way across the sky, painting it with hues of contemplation, Sarah acknowledged the duality of her journey—the ceaseless struggle between the search for intimacy and the defense of the self.

With the mantle of dusk upon the city, Sarah's silhouette melded with the lengthening shadows, a physical echo of the introspection that cloaked her mind. A distant siren wailed, a serenade to the closing of day and the unfurling of night's enigmatic tapestry. Tomorrow would be a testament to her choice, a crucible within which the mettle of her decision would be tested. But tonight, as she made her solitary way through the twilight, she took solace in the knowledge that, no matter what happens, she had stood unwavering in the face of adversity—a sentinel against the dark.

Chapter 14

Sarah Martin, the embodiment of resolve wrapped in a veneer of trepidation, found herself standing—no, rather, anchoring herself against the tremors of her own heartbeat—just inches from the unassuming wood of Bill Simmons' apartment door. The corridor, with its nondescript beige walls and the muffled sounds of life happening behind other, similar barriers, seemed to press in on her, as though it too anticipated the imminent unraveling of secrets.

Her fingers, which had danced across keyboards to compose symphonies of corporate strategy and motherly love notes alike, now hesitated, betraying the assuredness that usually radiated from her like warmth from an open flame. But this was no ordinary encounter, no routine exchange; it was the fulcrum upon which her future balance of trust and affection precariously teetered.

With lungs that felt constricted by the gravity of what lay ahead, Sarah inhaled deeply, drawing in the recycled air of the building as if it were the purest oxygen, willing it to infuse her with the fortitude necessary for the task at hand. It was a breath that sought to steel her spirit, to gird her will in a way that was reminiscent of ancient warriors pausing for a moment of silent reflection before the clash of battle.

Then, as the breath escaped her lips—a harbinger of the storm to come—her knuckles rapped against the door, a staccato testament to the collision course she had set herself upon. This was not just a physical act of summoning Bill from the sanctuary of his hidden truths; it was a metaphysical declaration that she would no longer be an unwitting passenger in their shared narrative.

Yes, there stood Sarah, a single mother whose very essence was an alloy of vulnerability and tenacity, poised on the cusp of confrontation and catharsis, knocking upon the door behind which waited not just a man, but the potential unraveling of a carefully woven tapestry of trust and intimacy.

The door swung open with a swift, almost imperceptible creak, revealing Bill's visage—a tableau of surprise etched with the faintest lines of suspicion. His eyes, those twin pools of cerulean mystery, narrowed ever so slightly as they bore into Sarah's, while his arms, crossed in a barricade of sinew and cloth across his chest, spoke an unspoken lexicon of defensiveness. He leaned against the doorframe, embodying the physical embodiment of a fortress at the ready, his posture telegraphing a man bracing for siege.

"Sarah?" The word tilted at the edges, pitched with incredulity and a dash of wariness, as though her very presence at his threshold was an aberration in the fabric of his expectations.

"Bill," she returned, letting his name hang between them like the opening gambit in a chess match where the stakes were measured not in kings and queens, but raw, unvarnished truths. "We need to talk."

"Talk?" Bill's voice, laced now with a tinge of scoffing humor that failed to reach his still guarded mine, betrayed the undercurrents of tension straining beneath the surface civility. "By all means, let us parley—though I suspect this will be less an exchange of pleasantries than a crucible wherein accusations are forged."

"Accusations? No, Bill. Facts," Sarah retorted, her words sharp as shards of glass, crystalline and cutting. "The kind that shatter illusions and lay bare the skeletons you've been hoarding behind closed doors."

"Ah, a purveyor of truths, then?" Bill countered, unfolding his arms with a fluid motion that belied the tightening coil of agitation within. "Come armed with revelations meant to flay the soul and expose its inner workings?"

"Flattery will get you nowhere," she shot back, her voice a fusillade of steely resolve and barely contained ire. "Your past—those dark chapters you conveniently omitted from our narrative—they're coming to light, whether you welcome their illumination or not."

"Dark chapters?" A laugh, bitter as wormwood, erupted from him, a sonic manifestation of derision. "You fancy yourself what? A sleuth? An arbiter of moral rectitude set upon exposing my alleged misdeeds?"

"Alleged?" Sarah's laugh was a mirror, reflecting his disdain with equal measure. "There's nothing alleged about it. The evidence is incontrovertible, even if your penchant for denial is as robust as your ego."

"Your so-called evidence," Bill sneered, his visage contorting momentarily into a mask of scorn before settling back into the calculated calm of a seasoned gambler bluffing his hand. "Wielded with the subtlety of a bludgeon, I presume, and as selectively curated as any despot's propaganda."

"Truth needs no curation," Sarah declared, her stance unwavering, even as her heart hammered a frenetic rhythm against her ribcage. "And I am done allowing you to play puppet master to a reality you've meticulously crafted out of lies and half-truths."

"Bravo," he applauded, slow claps dripping with sardonic applause. "A performance worthy of the stage. But let us not forget that in every play, there are two roles—victim and villain—and it seems you've cast me unequivocally as the latter."

"Roles can be deceiving," she said, her gaze unflinching. "But actions? They sing a chorus of authenticity that no amount of your posturing can silence."

"Indeed," he conceded, a cryptic smile playing at the corners of his mouth. "Then let the chorus sing, and we shall see whose tune carries the weight of truth."

Sarah unfurled the sheaf of papers with a flourish that seemed almost theatrical in the dim corridor. Her fingers, though trembling as if dancing to the silent tune of her roiling emotions, gripped the documents with a resoluteness that belied her inner turmoil. With each paper brandished like a battle standard before Bill's wary

eyes, her voice wove a tapestry of accusation—a blend of
stentorian authority and the raw timbre of wounded vulnerability.

"Here," she said, thrusting a photograph towards him, the corners
crinkling under the force of her conviction. "Look upon your
handiwork, the fingerprints of your fury left indelibly upon those
who once held you in affection's misguided embrace."

Bill recoiled as if the image seared his flesh, his countenance
morphing into a tableau of indignation and contempt. His lips
curled, not quite into a snarl, but with enough disdain to suggest
the proximity of such an expression.

"Melodrama does not become you, Sarah," he retorted, his voice
gaining an edge sharp enough to pare the truth down to convenient
slices. "Nor does playing the role of the avenging angel armed with
nothing but hearsay and conjecture."

"Conjecture?" The word escaped her lips steeped in incredulity,
laced with a bitter mirth that momentarily lit the gravity of their
parley. "These are testimonies, Bill. Voices that have been silenced
too long by fear and by the specter of your retribution."

"Testimonies bought and paid for, perhaps?" Bill suggested, the sly
tilt of his head indicating a game of chess played in the shadows,
where every move was cloaked in ambiguity. "Or simply the
fanciful creations of minds ensnared by the desire for vengeance or
the lure of lucre?"

"Neither bribes nor fantasies gave birth to these accounts," Sarah
asserted, her gaze locked onto his with an intensity that sought to
puncture the armor of his denial. "These words are born from pain
and the courage to rise above it—to expose the man behind the
mask."

"Ah, but masks," Bill mused, his tone taking on the lilting cadence of
a philosopher musing over the human condition, "are worn not
only to deceive others but to shield oneself from the glare of
unkind truths. Who is to say whose face is truly hidden?"

"Yours, Bill," Sarah pronounced with finality, each syllable heavy with the gravitas of judgment. "For beneath mine lies only the resolve to bring light to dark corners. And there," she paused, pointing at the stack of evidence, each page a silent witness, "lies the irrefutable legacy of your actions—no matter how fervently you deny them."

Sarah hesitated, the evidence clutched in her hands now a veritable Pandora's box, its contents threatening to unleash chaos upon the fragile world she had built. Her knuckles whitened around the sheaf of papers as she contemplated the chasm that yawned before her—a choice between the sanctity of truth and the preservation of a precarious happiness. The skin around her eyes tightened, a physical testament to the tempest of emotions swirling within.

"Bill," she began, her voice barely more than a whisper, betraying the internal siege laid upon her convictions, "you must understand the magnitude of what hangs in the balance here." A quiver danced upon her lips, the ballet of fear and fortitude played out in the subtle twitch of muscle and sinew. "The app... our creation—it stands to lose everything. Its integrity, the trust of its users; it's not just a platform, it's a promise we've made."

Her shoulders squared then, as if bracing against the gale of potential repercussions, her frame a bastion against an unseen onslaught. "I stand at the precipice, Bill, weighing the scales where on one side lies exposure, with all its excoriating light, and on the other, the somber shadow of silence." Sarah's arms unfolded; palms turned upward—a gesture embodying the stark duality of her choice.

"Silence is a shroud that suffocates truth, Sarah," Bill countered, his voice a blend of scorn and solemnity. "Yet, consider this: revelations such as these, once loosed into the world, are as wild stallions—uncontrollable, trampling reputations and relationships beneath their thunderous hooves."

"Indeed," she conceded, the corners of her mouth downturned in acknowledgment of the double-edged sword she wielded, "to reveal is to rend the very fabric we've woven together. It would cast a pall over the app, this vessel of communal aspirations, tainting it with the stain of personal failings."

Bill's gaze found hers, locking himself in a silent battle of wills. "And what of us, Sarah?" he asked, his words heavy with unspoken meaning. "This maelstrom you beckon forth—do you deem our nascent bond so frail that it cannot weather the storm?"

A sigh escaped her, a release of pent-up anxiety that carried with it an undercurrent of rueful mirth. "You credit our bond with the resilience of mythic lore when it's but in its infancy, still mewling for the comfort of trust's unbroken cradle." Her hand fluttered to her chest, resting above her pounding heart, a subtle but potent reminder of the personal stakes at play. "To act or not, either way, I stand to lose a part of myself—the architect of a dream or the guardian of conscience."

"Life," Bill intoned with a philosophical arch of his eyebrow, "is the art of navigating the labyrinthine complexities of such choices, each path fraught with its own brand of tribulation and triumph."

Sarah's laugh was a short, sharp sound, a bark of mirth tinged with the bitterness of irony. "Then may the minotaur of consequence find me a worthy adversary," she said, the quiver in her voice now replaced by the steel of resolve. "For I shall choose my battles with both eyes wide open, even if the fates decree that victory should taste akin to ashes in my mouth."

"Enough!" The word detonated in the charged air, a verbal shrapnel that shredded the last vestiges of civility between them. Sarah's voice, so often the epitome of controlled eloquence, now rang with the clarion call of indignation, each syllable a defiant flag unfurled against the gale of Bill's protests. Her hands clenched and unclenched as if grappling with the very fabric of reality, determined to reshape it to her will.

"Your words," she spat, "are but the sinuous dance of smoke, designed to obscure the scalding fire of truth." Her stance was that of a tempest incarnate, a maelstrom of emotion whirling within the confines of her formidable intellect.

"Truth?" Bill retorted; his tone serrated with scorn. "You wield it like a bludgeon, hoping to pummel me into submission, but I shall not be cowed by your self-righteous fervor." His arms unfolded from their defensive posture only to slash through the air, his gestures painting broad strokes of dissent in the canvas of their discourse.

"Self-righteous?" The laugh that escaped Sarah was devoid of humor, a hollow echo bouncing off the walls of reason and rebounding with incredulity. "If holding one accountable for the skeletons rattling in their closet is self-righteous, then let me wear the mantle with the unabashed pride of a paragon!"

In this verbal jousting, the thrust and parry of their argument rent the veil of congeniality that once swathed their relationship, exposing the raw underpinnings of vulnerability and suspicion. Could trust ever again bridge the chasm that yawned wide between them?

"Trust," Sarah murmured, more to herself than to Bill, her gaze drifting momentarily to some unseen horizon where hope might still glimmer faintly. "It is the currency of love, yet here we stand, you and I, bankrupted by the inflation of secrets and lies."

Bill's expression, a chiaroscuro of defiance and dismay, seemed at war with itself. "Love?" he echoed, a tinge of desperation creeping into his timbre. "What about love, Sarah? Does it not merit a chance to rise phoenix-like from the ashes of past transgressions?"

"Perhaps," she conceded, her heart a metronome struggling to keep time with the erratic tempo of her thoughts. "But can love truly flourish in soil sown with shards of broken trust? Can it weather the deluge of doubt that now pours upon us?"

The room seemed to shrink around them, the walls closing in as if to bear witness to the seismic shift occurring within the fault lines of their bond. Sarah felt the weight of her own uncertainties, ponderous and relentless, as they infiltrated the ramparts of her resolve.

"Can we?" The question hung between them, a three-word testament to the fragility of human connection when confronted with the specter of uncomfortable truths. And it was in the crucible of that silence that Sarah grappled with the duality of her desires—the yearning for love's sweet embrace and the compulsion to honor the sanctity of integrity.

Stepping through the threshold of Bill's apartment, Sarah's departure was a tacit admission that resolution had eluded them both; the door closed behind her with a soft click that resonated like the final note of an elegy for what might have been. Her silhouette, etched against the nascent twilight, bore the posture of one wrestling with an internal maelstrom, each droplet of the evening's cool air seeming to coalesce into a tangible aura of tumult around her.

Outside, the world continued unabated, the hum of the city a dissonant soundtrack to the disquiet churning within her. Sarah stood immobile, save for the gentle rise, and fall of her chest as she drew breaths that carried the weight of the universe. The labyrinthine corridors of her mind were alight with the ricochet of thoughts and emotions, each vying for supremacy in a battle where victory promised no true spoils.

In the chiaroscuro of streetlamps casting elongated shadows, Sarah's countenance was a study in contradiction—a visage carved from equal parts determination and despair, the furrow of her brow a testament to the gravity of her deliberation. With the heels of her hands pressed against her temples, as if to contain the cerebral tempest, she sought solace in the rhythmic pulsing of her own heartbeat, a metronomic reminder that life persists even amidst the cacophony of existential disarray.

The decision before her was not merely a fork in the road; it was a precipice, and whichever path she chose would irrevocably alter the trajectory of her journey. To expose Bill's veiled past was to potentially shatter the foundation of their app, a digital edifice constructed on the bedrock of trust and transparency. Yet, to remain silent was to become an accomplice to the shadows, to betray the very essence of the person she endeavored to be.

As she grappled with the Gordian knot of her predicament, Sarah's fingertips danced across the screen of her phone with an absent-minded cadence, a subconscious seeking of connection in an ocean of isolation. It was then, amidst the silence punctuated only by the distant siren song of the city, that the device sprang to life in her palm, its sudden vibration of a clarion call that sliced through her reverie.

A name flickered across the display, a harbinger of news or just another echo in the chamber of uncertainties. The identity of the caller hung suspended in the liquid crystal diorama, a portentous omen whose significance lay shrouded in potentiality. And as Sarah's thumb hovered over the answer button, the reader was left perched upon the precipice alongside her, peering into the abyss of what-ifs, their appetite for revelation whetted by the promise of an enigma yet to unfold.

Chapter 15

Sarah stared at the mountain of evidence spread across her dining room table. Printouts of abusive emails, screenshots of Bill's unsavory dating profiles, even signed statements of facts from past girlfriends detailing his manipulative behavior. She shook her head, still struggling to reconcile the charming man she'd come to care for with this monster in the making.

With a deep breath, she gathered the papers into a file folder. She would confront him with the truth. Give him a chance to explain, though she doubted any excuse would satisfy her.

The bustling coffee shop hummed with Saturday morning chatter. Sarah chose a table near the window, in full view of the baristas and patrons. She sipped her latte anxiously, rehearsing the speech in her mind.

Right on time, Bill strolled in. The same handsome smile that once made Sarah weak now turned her stomach. He approached with arms open for an embrace, but she stopped him with an outstretched hand.

"Have a seat," she said coldly. "We need to talk."

Confused, he sank into the chair across from her. She slid the folder over to him. He paged through it, brows knitted, as she detailed the contents: accounts of emotional abuse, threats against past partners. Proof he was not who he claimed to be.

Bill's face reddened. "This is absurd," he scoffed. "You can't actually believe these lies."

"I spoke to these women myself," Sarah said. "The patterns are clear. You need help."

He laughed bitterly. "So that's it? You've already condemned me over hearsay from strangers?"

Sarah held his accusing glare. She would not let him twist the narrative.

"I gave you a chance to explain," she said evenly. "You chose denial. I can't ignore these warning signs."

Bill stood abruptly, chair screeching against the tile. The coffee shop chatter faded to tense silence.

"You'll regret this," he growled under his breath.

Sarah stood as well. She matched his height, refusing to be intimidated.

"The only thing I regret is not exposing your abuse sooner," she replied. "Consider this your first and final warning."

Bill stormed out without another word, file folder in hand. The truth was out. Where it led, only time would tell. But Sarah walked out of that coffee shop with her head held high, integrity intact.

Sarah took a deep breath as she watched Bill storm out of the coffee shop. Though she had remained composed during the confrontation, her heart was pounding. She had taken a huge risk exposing his abusive past, but she knew it was the right thing to do.

As Sarah gathered her things and made for the exit, she thought back to how she had felt when she first met Bill. He had seemed charming, thoughtful, everything she wanted in a partner after her painful divorce. But the initial infatuation faded as worrisome rumors began trickling in from women in Bill's past.

Sarah realized she had two choices - ignore the red flags or seek the truth. Though it meant potentially losing a relationship, she knew she couldn't in good conscience ignore signs of abuse.

Now, having presented Bill with the damning evidence, the die was cast. Sarah had no idea how he would react or what he was capable of. But she refused to be intimidated into silence.

Stepping outside into the sunlight, Sarah lifted her face to the warm rays. She had spoken the truth. Though the path ahead was uncertain, she moved forward with integrity. For now, that was enough.

Sarah took a deep breath as she watched Bill storm out of the coffee shop, his face red with rage. Though she had remained composed during the confrontation, her heart was pounding. She had taken a huge risk exposing his abusive past, but she knew it was the right thing to do.

As Sarah gathered her things to leave, Bill suddenly burst back through the doors and marched straight up to her table. Sarah froze, her stomach lurching.

"You think you can threaten to ruin me and just walk away?" Bill seethed through clenched teeth. "I built my reputation through years of hard work. You have no idea who you're dealing with."

He leaned over the table, his piercing blue eyes boring into hers. Sarah forced herself not to flinch.

"I tried to let you down easily," he continued. "But you just had to keep digging. Well congratulations, you just made a very dangerous enemy."

Sarah stood up slowly, summoning every ounce of courage. "I exposed the truth, Bill. If your reputation suffers, you have only yourself to blame."

Bill slammed his fist on the table, causing Sarah's coffee to slosh over the rim. The other patrons went silent, watching the confrontation unfold.

"I have connections, Sarah," Bill said, his voice low and menacing. "Powerful connections. I could destroy your career, ruin that pathetic little app you worked so hard on."

Sarah felt her confidence faltering. She had expected backlash, but not outright threats. Her mind raced as she weighed the risks of taking Bill down versus protecting her livelihood.

Sensing her hesitation, Bill pressed his advantage. "But it doesn't have to be that way. We can forget this unfortunate incident ever happened." He gently brushed a strand of hair from her face. "In fact, I think you and I could be very good for each other."

Sarah shuddered, then quickly stepped back from his touch. She had to be strong now, for all the women who endured worse at Bill's hands.

"I will never be silenced or intimidated," she declared. "Now get out before I call the police."

Bill's eyes narrowed to slits. Without another word, he turned and stormed out, almost knocking over a server. Sarah watched him go, knowing this was far from over.

Sarah took a deep breath to steady her nerves. She had made her decision - Bill's abusive behavior could not continue, no matter the personal consequences.

First, she compiled all the evidence into a dossier: the screenshots of inappropriate messages, testimonies from former partners detailing emotional manipulation, even photos of bruises sent discreetly. It was damning proof of a disturbing pattern of domestic violence.

Next, Sarah contacted Maggie Robinson, an investigative journalist known for exposing corrupt public figures. She was perfect for an explosive exposé on Bill.

"I have everything you need to bring this abuser to justice," Sarah said as she met Maggie in a quiet corner of a local park. She handed over the dossier.

Maggie flipped through it, her expression growing graver. "This is huge," she said finally. "We'll need to move quickly before he can do more damage control."

They hashed out a plan to break the story simultaneously across print, digital, and social media for maximum impact. Sarah knew the community backlash would be intense, but she steeled herself for the storm ahead.

Three days later, the story detonated like a bomb. The app's servers almost crashed from the influx of traffic as people rushed to read about Bill's years of calculated manipulation and violence.

Reactions ranged from outraged too skeptical. Some questioned Sarah's motives, but many more praised her courage. Bill retreated from the public eye, but the extent of the damage was yet to be seen. For now, Sarah had taken the stand she knew was right, whatever the cost. Justice had been served.

Sarah knew Bill would not take this public shaming lightly. She expected retaliation but was still shocked by how quickly it came.

The next morning, a flood of one-star reviews tanked the app's rating overnight. Then came an onslaught of fake news articles popping up online, spreading wild conspiracy theories about Sarah and questioning the app's integrity.

It was a deliberate smear campaign, and Bill's fingerprints were all over it. He was trying to undermine everything Sarah had built.

She called an emergency meeting with Jason and the other moderators. "Bill is trying to sabotage us," she said grimly. "But we won't let him win."

They got to work immediately. Jason strengthened their firewalls and implemented new security protocols to guard against cyber-attacks. The moderators flagged hundreds of fake reviews and articles, working late into the night.

Slowly, steadily, they regained control. The app's true supporters rallied around Sarah. They flooded her inbox with words of encouragement and took to social media to defend the app against Bill's lies.

Sarah was moved to tears by these acts of solidarity. It gave her the strength to keep fighting, no matter how hard Bill tried to tear them down. She wouldn't let him ruin this community that meant so much to her.

After a week of nonstop vigilance, the worst of the attacks died down. Bill's campaign to destroy the app had failed. He realized that the truth was more powerful than his deceit.

Sarah knew he might try again, but she was prepared. Bill had lost this battle. Her app would survive, its mission more important than ever.

Sarah called a meeting of the support group moderators. As they gathered in her living room, she saw the toll this ordeal had taken - there were dark circles under their eyes and a weary tension in their shoulders. But their determination remained strong.

"I know it's been an exhausting few weeks," Sarah began. "Bill's sabotage attempts have shaken our community's trust. But we will regain it, one day at a time."

Murmurs of assent rippled through the group. Myra, a single mother of three, spoke up. "No matter what Bill throws at us, we'll be here. This app changed my life. I finally felt safe dating again after my divorce."

Others chimed in with similar sentiments. Sarah was moved by their steadfast loyalty. This app was so much more than a business to them - it represented hope.

"We'll need to be vigilant," said Jason, always the pragmatic one. "Bill clearly has connections and resources. I've added more firewalls, but he could strike again."

Sarah nodded. "You're right. We can't let our guard down. But we also can't lose sight of why we're here. Our community needs this app. Now more than ever, we have to keep it safe for single parents."

Resolve shone on the faces around her. No matter the challenges ahead, Sarah knew they would face them together. Bill had dealt them a blow, but he hadn't defeated them.

As the meeting ended, Sarah felt a swell of gratitude. With the support of this group by her side, she could withstand anything Bill threw her way. They would restore trust in the app, step by step. Its mission was too important to fail.

Sarah took a deep breath as the others filed out of the room. The meeting had gone better than she expected, but there was still a knot in her stomach.

This was her baby - she had poured her heart and soul into creating this app. And now, thanks to Bill's sabotage, its reputation was in tatters.

She slumped down in a chair, rubbing her temples. Self-doubt crept in. Had she made a mistake exposing Bill so publicly? Maybe if she had handled it more delicately, they wouldn't be in this mess.

"Hey," said Jason, resting a hand on her shoulder. "No second-guessing yourself. You did the right thing."

Sarah gave a wan smile. "I hope so. I just wish..."

"I know," he said. "But we'll get through this, one day at a time. Now come on, we've got an app to rebuild."

He offered his hand and pulled Sarah to her feet. As they walked out together, she felt her resolve strengthening. With her friends by her side, she would make it through this storm.

Bill had tested her, but he hadn't broken her. She was stronger than he realized. And she would never stop fighting for what mattered - not just this app, but the single parent community who needed it.

Her head held high; Sarah stepped out to face the challenges ahead.

Chapter 16

Sarah perched on the edge of her velveteen sofa, an island of solitude, in the sprawling sea of her dimly lit living room. The soft glow from a solitary lamp threw her shadow against the walls — a stark silhouette marred by the furrows of consternation deeply etched upon her brow. She was momentarily a statue, save for the rhythmic rise and fall of her chest, each breath a silent testament to the tumultuous thoughts that besieged her mind. In these quiet hours, she grappled with the Sisyphean task of safeguarding her digital brainchild, a mobile application designed as a bastion for single parents venturing into the fraught world of online dating. Her creation, once a beacon of hope, now seemed like a vessel navigating treacherous waters, with the safety of its passengers resting squarely upon her shoulders.

A sudden spasm of resolve tightened her grip, her knuckles whitening as if trying to wring out the dark doubts that clouded her judgement. Was she, Sarah Martin, truly the custodian of these vulnerable hearts? The gravity of her responsibility bore down upon her with an almost palpable weight, tethering her spirit to a carousel of quandaries that spun ceaselessly. Her formidable will, which had always been her compass through life's unpredictable squalls, now flickered under the shadow of an insidious question: could she, amidst the cacophony of cyber threats and duplicitous avatars, erect a fortress robust enough to shield others from the perilous gambits of online courtship?

Her humor, typically as resilient as tempered steel, found no purchase in the irony that she, who sought to architect connections between kindred souls, now confronted an indomitable adversary in her own quest for communal safety. The jest that life often played, thrusting the protector into the throes of vulnerability, did not escape her; yet it elicited not a chuckle but a steely determination to wrest control from the jaws of uncertainty.

In that moment of clenched resolve, Sarah's intellect, ever the agile acrobat, pirouetted around the conundrum, refusing to succumb to the paralysis of fear. Her vision, though momentarily clouded by the specter of failure, began to sharpen with the clarity that only those who have weathered storms can truly possess. It was within this crucible of self- doubt and introspection that Sarah Martin, a paragon of maternal vigilance and tenacious spirit, would either forge a new path or falter beneath the weight of her own aspirations.

Sarah's eyes, those twin beacons of determination now dimmed by the gravity of her task, swept over the room, and found anchorage on the soft glow of her laptop screen. There it was, her digital progeny, a mosaic of pixels that harbored the collective hopes of hearts seeking companionship amidst the solitary journey of single parenthood. The interface, with its sleek design and intuitive touch, beckoned like a lighthouse to the weary traveler, promising safe harbor in a sea churned by the capricious winds of romance.

She exhaled slowly, a deliberate breath that carried the weight of her burden, as if willing it into the ether of her quiet abode. The air that filled her lungs also ballooned her resolve; she would not—could not—allow herself to be submerged in doubt. With each rhythmic inhale and exhale, Sarah's mind waltzed through the labyrinth of code and feature, each step a measured tread amidst the potential minefield of exploitation.

"Could there be a chink," she mused, "a fissure so minute yet so profound, within this virtual bastion I've erected?" Her thoughts pirouetted around Bill, the enigmatic suitor whose charm held a tincture of the unknown, a reminder that even the most unassailable fortress might fall if the enemy were, but a Trojan horse clad in an alluring guise. His presence in her life—a silhouette on the horizon—cast a long shadow over the fruits of her labor, seeding her mind with the chilling possibility of oversight.

Yes, the app was her citadel, a digital demesne where the tender narratives of single parents unfolded with cautious optimism. Yet even the mightiest castles had their secret passages, their hidden weaknesses known only to the astute or the malevolent. It was this thought that ensnared Sarah's intellect, a Gordian knot that required not brute force but the incisive edge of wit to unravel.

In this silent chamber of introspection, she stood sentinel over her creation, a guardian whose vigilance was as much a shield against the external as it was a bulwark against the internal tempests of apprehension. With the tenacity of a cartographer charting unexplored realms, Sarah prepared to embark upon a meticulous odyssey through the app's architecture, each line of code a potential Rosetta Stone to thwart the cunning of those who, like Bill, might harbor ulterior motives beneath a veneer of sincerity.

And so it was that Sarah Martin, cloaked in the armor of her intellect and armed with the sabra of her humor, stood ready to defend the realm she had built—not just for herself, but for the legion of single parents who had entrusted her with their dreams of a love both steadfast and secure.

The cursor blinked mockingly on the screen—a solitary sentry amidst a fortress of algorithms and firewalls that Sarah had painstakingly constructed. Yet now, its regular rhythm echoed the drumbeat of discontent that had been surfacing with increasing regularity in her inbox. The very measures she had implemented to safeguard the vulnerable hearts of single parents seeking solace and companionship within the digital confines of her app were now being branded as overreaching by a vocal minority. Her commitment to security, once lauded, now faced scrutiny under the myopic lens of convenience.

"Too much," they said. "Too invasive," they complained. These words reverberated through the caverns of her resolve, seeding doubts where once there stood unassailable conviction. Had she, in her quest to fortify against the prowling predators of the online dating world, erected barriers so imposing that even genuine affection could not scale them? The balance between vigilance and accessibility teetered precariously on the fulcrum of public opinion, and Sarah, custodian of this delicate equilibrium, felt the weight of potential error press upon her like the leaden cloak of Atlas himself.

A sigh escaped her lips, transmuting into a silent laugh devoid of any humor—a wry acknowledgment of the paradox that often accompanies pioneering ventures. In a gesture born of restive energy, she ran her fingers through the cascade of dark hair that framed her face, each strand slipping through like the myriad thoughts trying to escape the confines of her focused mind. The specter of vulnerability loomed large, casting long shadows over the landscape of her intentions. A breach, should it ever occur, was a chasm too ghastly to contemplate. Not just for the edifice of credibility she had built around her professional persona, but for the real, flesh-and-blood individuals whose trust was the keystone of her enterprise.

Her reputation was a mosaic of tenacity and acumen, yet it paled in comparison to the responsibility she bore towards her clientele. Single parents, who had already navigated the labyrinthine trials of heartache and hope, now traversed her digital domain in search of a kindred spirit to share the quotidian joys and tribulations of their lives. The thought of their trust being betrayed under her watch stirred a tempest in the vessel of her soul—waves of accountability crashing against the hull of her determination.

In the crucible of her musings, Sarah understood that the alchemy of fear and responsibility could either yield a paralyzing toxin or the elixir of innovation. The choice lay squarely in her capable hands, hands that had coded pathways to connection, hands that now hovered above the keyboard, ready to forge new bulwarks to protect the realm she had vowed to defend.

Sarah's eyes, those twin beacons of resolve now dimmed by the creeping fog of uncertainty, flitted across the room like sparrows in a gale. Each ornament and photo, every book on the shelf seemed to mock her with their silent permanence, as if they were guardians to answers that spun just out of reach. The notion of enlisting external expertise tiptoed through her mind—a seductive siren call tempting her to relinquish a fragment of control in exchange for fortification. Yet, within the crucible of her self-reliance, she pondered whether the tools for transcendence lay not in external salvation but in the untapped reservoirs of her own ingenuity.

As this internal colloquy unfolded, a nascent spark ignited behind the steely curtain of Sarah's gaze—her visage a canvas where defeat wrestled with resurgence. Memories of the support group, that consortium of kindred spirits each grappling with the symbiotic dance of hope and vulnerability, fanned the ember of her resolve. Their collective belief in her, more steadfast than the North Star, pierced the shroud of her doubts. These allies, who had navigated their own odysseys of single parenthood, had anchored their faith not in the app itself but in the woman who wielded it like a shield against the capricious whims of fate.

The recollection of their words, each a buoyant lifeline cast into the roiling sea of her trepidations, bestowed upon her a shimmering filament of hope. It was as though their trust and companionship were alchemical ingredients in the transformative potion she so desperately sought. This fellowship, bound not by mere digital threads but by the unspoken oath to safeguard the sanctity of their shared journey, breathed life into the embers of her determination, coaxing it into a flame that could illuminate the path forward.

Sarah's fingers, once listless in her lap, now moved with purpose as she retrieved the slim beacon of connection from its resting place beside her. The familiar coolness of the phone's surface was a tactile anchor to reality, a stark counterpoint to the warmth of human sentiment soon to cascade from its screen. With a few deft swipes, she summoned the digital tapestry of messages that wove together the narratives of hearts similarly situated in the precarious limbo between longing and fulfillment.

The glowing pixels coalesced into words of sustenance, each message a testament to the shared odyssey that underpinned their virtual conclave. Here lay the written echoes of laughter that had bounced off the walls of adversity, the empathetic embrace of those who knew the labyrinthine challenges of single parenthood not as abstract hurdles but as intimate familiars. Sarah's eyes absorbed the text, each sentence a brushstroke on the mural of collective resilience that adorned the support group's digital alcove.

"Your app is a lighthouse in the fog of the dating world," one message read, its metaphor a salve to Sarah's flagging spirits. Another chimed in, "It's the armor I never knew I needed," a declaration that lent gravity to her resolve. These were not mere platitudes; they were the reflections of lives touched and trajectories altered by the fruit of her labor—a labor born not out of mere code and algorithm but of a deeply rooted desire to forge a bulwark against the treacherous tides of chance encounters.

As the montage of heartfelt missives continued to unfurl before her, Sarah could feel the tendrils of doubt begin to retreat, usurped by a burgeoning sense of camaraderie. It dawned upon her with the gentle insistence of a sunrise that her journey was interlaced with the journeys of others—each individual thread contributing to the tensile strength of an invisible web that spanned the expanse of their collective experience.

This network, this cadre of solo navigators, was more than an assembly of disparate souls seeking companionship; it was a fellowship, a mutualistic symbiosis where support flowed as readily as the currents in a vast ocean, and every member buoyed the others against the relentless swells. With this epiphany, the specter of isolation that had haunted Sarah's thoughts dissipated like mist at the behest of a burgeoning dawn. She was a vital node within a nexus of solidarity, each member unified in the quest for affection and safety, their shared vulnerabilities the very mortar binding them in resolute alliance.

Together, they stood as a phalanx against the myriad challenges that would dare encroach upon their citadel of trust. In recognizing the collective power that surged through this interconnected web of single parents, Sarah grasped a fundamental truth—their unity was a panacea to her solitary apprehensions, a chalice brimming with the elixir of communal fortitude. With this realization cradling her spirit, Sarah felt the weight on her shoulders alchemize into wings, ready to soar above the fray and conquer the unknown with the might of many.

With the steadfast tenacity of a seasoned cartographer charting unknown territories, Sarah's fingers danced across the laptop's keyboard, each tapping an echo of her resolve. The screen glowed like a beacon in the dimly lit room, its luminescence casting a spectral aura around her as she delved into the digital archives and forums that held the secrets to fortifying her app's bulwarks. She was a solitary sentinel in this quiet hour, her mission clear and her spirit undeterred by the Sisyphean task at hand.

The cursor blinked rhythmically, a silent metronome to her thoughts as it navigated through cascades of data and scholarly articles on cybersecurity. She absorbed information with the voracity of a bibliophile in the hallowed halls of an ancient library, each piece of knowledge a tessera in the mosaic she was determined to complete. Her mind, a crucible of innovation, simmered with ideas, synthesizing abstract theories and concrete strategies with alchemical finesse.

As she plunged deeper into the intricacies of encryption algorithms and two-factor authentication protocols, the vestiges of doubt that once gnawed at the edges of her confidence began to dissolve. In their stead blossomed a sense of purpose so profound it seemed to resonate within the very marrow of her bones. This was not merely a professional endeavor; it was a crusade for the safeguarding of hearts seeking solace in companionship, a testament to her unwavering commitment to the tribe of single parents who had placed their trust in her vision.

Sarah knew that the mantle she bore was laden with responsibilities, its fabric interwoven with the delicate threads of hope and the steely fibers of vigilance. But within the crucible of her resolve, fears were transmuted into fuel that stoked the fires of her determination. No longer was she the daunted soul wrestling with the specter of failure; she emerged as the architect of a fortress designed to shield against the insidious wolves that prowled the digital woods.

It was a battle waged on a frontier unseen but no less treacherous than any physical battlefield, and Sarah Martin—single mother, innovator, protector—stood ready at the gates, armed not with sword and shield, but with intellect and empathy. She was more than an engineer of code; she was a guardian of dreams, and with every keystroke, she etched her defiance against the odds into the annals of a world braving the tides of change.

Sarah's fingers danced a frenetic tarantella across the keyboard, orchestrating a symphony of digital safeguards as she meticulously drafted her magnum opus of a security plan. It was an intricate blueprint, weaving additional layers of verification into the very fabric of the app, each line of code a bulwark against the cunning machinations of predators like Bill. Her mind buzzed with fervent activity, neurons firing like a well-oiled Gatling gun as she pieced together the puzzle of protection with the finesse of a seasoned cryptologist.

For Sarah, this was no mere tinkering at the edges of cybersecurity; it was a full-scale revolution in the making. She envisioned a fortress impregnable, replete with moats of multi-factor authentication and battlements bristling with the latest in encryption technology. Each new measure was a testament to her tenacity, a gauntlet thrown down in the face of those who dared challenge the sanctity of her digital realm.

With the blueprint etched into the virtual ether, Sarah paused—a brief intermission in her one-woman crusade—to marshal the forces of her support group. She crafted a missive with the precision of an expert wordsmith, its contents charged with the electricity of her resolve. The message was a clarion call to arms, an invitation for her fellow guardians to lend their might to the fortification efforts. Her plea was not that of a supplicant but a general rallying her troops for the skirmishes ahead.

"Esteemed allies," she began, infusing her text with the gravitas of her newfound determination, "our bastion stands poised on the precipice of evolution. I beseech your counsel and your valor as we endeavor to erect defenses that rival the mythical walls of yore. Together, we shall sculpt a sanctuary that laughs in the face of peril, a citadel where the hearts of single parents may cavort free from the shadow of trepidation."

The message soared through the digital ether, an electronic falcon dispatched with tidings of unity and shared purpose. Sarah knew that the collective wisdom of her support group— those valiant souls who had weathered similar storms—would be instrumental in buttressing the ramparts of their common enterprise. In their fellowship, she found the alchemy that transmuted solitary struggle into communal triumph.

So, there it was, the die cast, the gauntlet picked up; a convocation of kindred spirits bound by the noblest of quests. Sarah sat back in her chair, the ghost of a smile playing upon her lips—a rare fusion of humor amidst gravity—as she awaited the echoes of assent from her digital round table.

The unmistakable click of Sarah's laptop closing reverberated through the room, a definitive punctuation to her marathon of digital fortification. Her eyes, those twin sentinels that had stood vigilant over the glowing battlefield of her computer screen, now shone with an incipient fire—the harbinger of hope in the face of a Sisyphean task. There sat Sarah Martin, erstwhile warrior of the web, whose once-flagging spirits now found themselves buoyed by an invisible yet palpable tide.

It was not merely the echo of triumph from the recently dispatched missive to her cyber cohort that sparked this nascent optimism. No, it was something more akin to the alchemist's elusive elixir that turns base metals into precious gold. Here was a woman who had stared into the abyss of online vulnerability, only to see her own reflection gazing back with unrelenting resolve. She understood, with crystalline clarity, that the road ahead would be strewn with obstacles as formidable as the labyrinthine puzzles of Daedalus himself. Yet, she felt within her the stirring of an adamantine will, tempered in the forge of adversity, and quenched in the waters of communal support.

With a single, fluid motion, Sarah pushed herself away from the table, her chair receding like a trusty steed having borne its rider valiantly through the throes of battle. She stood alone, yet not solitary, bolstered by the unseen phalanx of single parents who shared her vision—a legion of hearts seeking amour sans peril. The air around her seemed to thrum with the silent chorus of their collective determination, a symphony of intent that transformed her doubt into a sword of purpose.

A wry smile played upon her lips, the kind that spoke of inner jests shared only with oneself, as she recognized the duality of her quest. Here was Sarah, the quintessential champion of love's tender cause, armed with naught but her wits and the unwavering belief of those whom she sought to protect. Love, that most capricious of foes, now had an unlikely ally in the form of lines of code, protocols, and virtual battlements designed to ward off the specters of deceit and malice.

As the final light of day yielded to the encroaching twilight, Sarah's silhouette was etched against the dimming luminescence of her living room, a tableau vivant of resolve. Her journey, she knew, was far from over; it was just beginning. Yet, in this quiet moment of introspection, Sarah Martin—single mother, sentinel of safety, architect of amorous aspirations—embraced the challenges that lay ahead with a heart fortified by the very thing she endeavored to safeguard: the indomitable human spirit.

Chapter 17

Sarah Martin swept into the local coffee shop with a kinetic energy that swirled the very air around her, the door chiming a quaint but assertive welcome as she navigated through the maze of tables and chairs. Her eyes, those vigilant sentinels perpetually scanning for both opportunity and threat, found Jason Clark ensconced in a corner booth, his figure hunched over a laptop like a modern-day alchemist engrossed in the quest to transmute binary code into digital gold.

"Good to see you've already set up base camp," Sarah quipped as she slid into the seat opposite him, her laptop, and notebooks an arsenal of ideas ready to unleash.

"Wouldn't miss it for the world," Jason replied, pushing his glasses up the bridge of his nose with a finger, a gesture emblematic of his readiness to dive into the task at hand. They were not merely friends but comrades-in-arms against the insidious specter of cyber insecurity that loomed over their creation.

Their mission was clear: fortify the app to be the bastion of safety in the tempestuous sea of online dating. As they began to dissect the current state of their creation, it was as if they were surgeons peeling back layers to expose vulnerabilities—each loophole a wound that needed suturing, each glitch a pathology demanding remedy.

"Two-factor authentication," Sarah intoned, her voice a mixture of revelation and resolve. The suggestion hung in the air between them, charged with the gravity of its implications. It was a beacon of hope, a clarion call to action that bespoke her innate understanding that in this digital age, one's identity was akin to a castle that must be guarded with the fiercest of vigilance.

"Ah, the vaunted drawbridge of verification," Jason mused, his humor lacing his acknowledgment with the levity that belied the seriousness of their endeavor. "Let us then lay siege to the usurpers of authenticity and reclaim the sanctum of our users' trust."

As they delved deeper into the strategic machinations required to implement such a feature, their dialogue became a duet of intellects, a symphony of synapses firing in harmony. With every potential solution they brainstormed, they wove a stronger net in which they hoped to capture any would-be digital marauders, ensuring that the sanctuary they provided for single parents would be impregnable.

And so, the scene was set, the players poised, and the plan of action unfurling before them like a blueprint to a more secure future.

Jason, his gaze affixed to the radiant dance of pixels on his laptop screen, embarked upon the arduous odyssey of coding with a zeal that was both infectious and intimidating. His fingers, agents of his will, tap-danced across the keyboard with the precision of a maestro coaxing harmonies from a piano. He delved into the labyrinthine recesses of the app's infrastructure, untangling the complex web of code with the deftness of a digital virtuoso. The implementation of two-factor authentication was not merely a task—it was a crusade against the specters of insecurity that haunted their digital realm.

With each passing hour, Jason's eyes remained undimmed by the scintillating glow of the screen, his focus unwavering as he wove the new security measure into the fabric of the app. It was as if he were crafting an incantation, a series of arcane rules designed to conjure a barrier impervious to the onslaught of nefarious entities. And when at last he initiated the testing phase, it was with the quiet confidence of an inventor who had just given life to a wondrous contraption, one that promised to safeguard the personal sanctuaries of their users.

In parallel, Sarah, whose determination was the bedrock upon which their endeavor stood, marshaled her considerable acumen in pursuit of enhancing the app's background check process. Her phone cradled between shoulder and ear; she orchestrated a partnership with a third-party agency renowned for their meticulous scrutiny. She negotiated with the finesse of a seasoned diplomat, her words carefully chosen, her intent unyielding. She sought not just a service but an alliance, one founded on the mutual understanding that the stakes were as high as the heavens—the safety and trust of every single parent who dared to seek companionship through their platform.

The negotiations were a ballet of proposals and counterproposals, each step measured, each turn executed with strategic grace. Sarah's goal was clear: to construct a bastion of reliability, to offer thorough and dependable screenings that would stand as a testament to their unwavering commitment to user safety. The agency, recognizing the nobility of her cause, acquiesced, and thus the pact was sealed, a bulwark against the uncertainties that fluttered like shadows in the corners of online interaction.

As the sun dipped below the horizon, painting the sky with hues of fading gold, the coffee shop around them simmered down to a murmur of languid activity. Sarah and Jason, their endeavors for the day reaching a natural denouement, leaned back in their chairs. Their screens glowed with the fruits of their labor—a beacon of diligence and innovation, illuminating the path toward a future where love could be pursued without fear, and trust could be built on the unshakable foundation of security.

Fingers dancing across the keyboard with a deftness born of years navigating the digital labyrinth, Jason's eyes remained locked on the screen, his gaze as steady as a surgeon's hand. Beside him, Sarah, whose mental cogs were whirring at a comparable RPM, mapped out the interface design with the finesse of an architect drafting blueprints for a monument destined to stand the test of time. They were in the throes of creation; each click and keystroke a chisel shaping the marble of their combined vision.

"Consideration must be given to the ease with which a single mother, already ensnared in the daily rigmarole of life's relentless demands, can interact with this platform," Sarah mused aloud, her tone imbued with the gravitas of her protective instincts. The interface before them was blooming into existence—a user-focused portal that married simplicity with sophistication, ensuring that anyone, regardless of their technological acumen, could navigate the waters of their personal data with the assurance of a seasoned captain.

"Transparency is paramount," Jason agreed, his voice carrying the warm timbre of one who appreciates the finer intricacies of human-computer symbiosis. "We shall create a digital pantheon where information is not merely presented but bestowed upon our users with the clarity of a mountain spring."

Their collaboration was akin to a symphonic duet, each movement synchronized with the other's, their thoughts converging like tributaries into the mighty river of their shared endeavor. As the interface took shape, it became clear that they were not only codifying lines of programming but inscribing a covenant of trust between the app and its patrons.

As if summoned by the gravity of their mission, Sarah's phone chimed with messages that twinkled like stars against the encroaching twilight of doubt. Members of the support group, those kindred spirits bound by the commonality of their solo parenting voyages, were dispatching digital missives of encouragement. "Your efforts are the armor in which our hearts will venture forth once more," read one, the words resonating within Sarah's chest like a drumbeat urging her onward.

"Behold the power of community," she declared, a smile playing upon her lips as the chorus of support emboldened her resolve. These affirmations served as a wind fill to her sails, reminding her that the quest they embarked upon bore the weight of countless hopes— hopes that were now, through her hands, being woven into the very fabric of the app.

"Let us forge ahead," Sarah said, her voice a clarion call that reverberated through the quietude of the coffee shop, now a bastion of their aspirations. With the support group's words as their anthem, Sarah and Jason leaned into their work, each line of code a verse in the poem of security they were composing for the single parents who would entrust them with their hearts' most vulnerable whispers.

Sarah flexed her fingers, digits wearied by keystrokes that seemed to stretch across an epoch, as they embarked upon the Sisyphean task of coaxing disparate systems into a harmonious duet. The background check feature, obstinate as it was, resisted integration into the app's delicate ecosystem like an ill-tempered rhinoceros refusing the yoke. The code, once a beacon of clarity, now morphed into an enigmatic tapestry, weaving frustration into every line.

"Curse these digital gremlins," Jason muttered under his breath, his eyes scanning lines of text with the intensity of a hawk surveilling its terrain. Sarah, too, felt the creeping tendrils of exasperation as the hours waned, each failed attempt to chip away at their reservoirs of optimism.

Yet, amidst this digital quagmire, Sarah's mind danced with the messages of the support group, their words a buoyant life raft amidst the tempest of coding chaos. Their faith, an invisible yet palpable force, galvanized her spirit. She could not—would not—allow their trust to be marooned upon the shores of disappointment.

"Jason," she declared, the timbre of her voice a blend of fortitude and assurance, "let's approach this conundrum with the presumption that our very logic is flawed. Let's dissect our assumptions and rebuild them from the foundation."

It was a gambit that demanded the deconstruction of their work, akin to an artist reimagining a masterpiece from the ground up. And so, with meticulous scrutiny, they embarked on the painstaking process of debugging, untangling the Gordian knot of algorithms and protocols that governed the app's inner sanctum.

Through the fusion of Sarah's methodical strategy and Jason's technical prowess, they unraveled the labyrinth, piece by intricate piece. Finally, as the clock heralded the arrival of a new morn, the solution emerged, elegant in its simplicity—a digital phoenix rising from the ashes of their perseverance.

"Victory!" Jason exclaimed, a triumphant grin splitting his features as the background check system seamlessly slotted into place, a testament to their tenacity.

With the two-factor authentication and the newly integrated background check features secured, they turned their focus to rigorous testing. Precision was paramount, for their creation was not merely an app but a bastion of safety in the unpredictable realm of online dating.

"Commence the trial by fire," Sarah said, her command mobilizing their next phase of action. They reached out to the stalwart members of the support group, inviting them to partake in the crucible of testing. These individuals were not mere users; they were the vanguards of the single parent community, each with a personal stake in the impregnable fortification of their shared digital sanctuary.

The feedback rolled in, a cascade of insights and observations that were invaluable to the fine-tuning of the app. With each suggestion implemented, a bug squashed, or a user interface polished, the app edged closer to becoming the paragon of security they envisioned. Sarah and Jason, alchemists of code, transformed the raw material of data and algorithms into a gleaming shield of protection, ready to safeguard the hearts and hopes of those embarking on journeys to find connection amidst the stars.

Sarah, tapping a rhythmic staccato on the mahogany table, surveyed the assembly of support group members with an astute gaze that missed no nuance in their expectant faces. Jason, ensconced beside her with his laptop aglow, cleared his throat — a digital-age herald ready to trumpet their victory over technological duress.

"Esteemed guardians of our collective endeavor," Sarah began, her voice a melodic blend of command and compassion, "we stand before you not as mere architects of software but as fellow sentinels, vigilant against the ever-looming specter of cyber malfeasance."

With a flourish of keystrokes, Jason projected the app's new features onto the screen. The two-factor authentication process gleamed like a digital sentinel at the gates of user safety, while the robust background check feature unfurled its intricate tapestry of security threads, each more tightly woven than the last.

"Your identities," Sarah continued, "once as vulnerable as ships adrift in an unforgiving digital sea, are now ensconced within the fortress of our making. The sanctity of your personal histories shall remain inviolate, safeguarded by layers of encryption and the vigilant eyes of our third-party sentries."

A murmur of approval rustled through the room, like leaves whispering secrets to the wind. Their gratitude, palpable as the warmth of a sunbeam, washed over Sarah, fueling the embers of her dedication into a blaze of resolve.

"Your commendations," she responded, inclining her head with solemn grace, "are the very sinew and substance that fortify our purpose."

In that moment, the partnership between developer and user was re-forged, stronger, and more resolute than ever before.

As the meeting drew to a close, and the last of the heartfelt accolades dwindled to companionable silence, Sarah and Jason initiated the digital missive that would herald the new dawn of their creation. With each click, they dispatched the update into the ether, a beacon calling all users to partake in the fruits of their labor.

"Behold," Jason announced, his voice suffused with a quiet pride, "the proclamation of our renewed vigilance. Let it be known that we have girded this domain with diligence and innovation. We beseech you, noble users, to wield these enhancements with care and to remit unto us your observations, that we may continue to refine our bulwark against the unseen adversary."

The update, a meticulous manifesto of the changes wrought, cascaded across the screens of devices everywhere, an invitation to engage with the transformed landscape of their digital interaction.

"Should the smallest discrepancy arise," Sarah intoned, "dispatch your clarion call to our attentive ears. Together, we shall uphold the bastion of trust that is the foundation upon which this platform stands."

And thus, with a shared vision of unwavering protection, Sarah and Jason cast their gaze toward the horizon, where the future beckoned with the promise of safe passage through the boundless realms of connection.

Bathed in the luminescent glow of screens pulsating with the vitality of a digital renaissance, Sarah Martin sat ensconced within the fortress of her meticulous design, her fingers dancing across the keys with a rhythmic staccato that bespoke the fervor of her labor. Jason Clark, her compatriot in this crusade for cyber-sentinels, monitored the influx of feedback with the keen eye of an eagle surveying its dominion.

"Behold," exclaimed Jason, his voice a timbre of bemused satisfaction, "the populace rejoices in our toils. Missives of commendation pour forth like libations upon the altar of security."

Sarah leaned in, peering at the cascade of notifications with a discerning gaze that missed naught. The users, those intrepid navigators of the app's amorous waters, had taken to the new features with a zeal that was heartening to witness. They penned their plaudits with the warmth of kindred spirits who had found solace in the safeguarded harbors of the platform.

"Indeed, we have struck a chord—an anthem resounding through the ether, heralding the dawn of vigilance," she mused, her lips curving into a smile that was both triumphant and tinged with irony. Their endeavor, born of trials and suffused with tenacity, had kindled the beacon of assurance for the legion of single parents whose quest for companionship was fraught with trepidation.

As the day waned, yielding to the embrace of twilight, the reverberations of their success rippled outward, catching the attention of the ever-watchful sentinels of the media. A local news outlet, renowned for its perspicacious coverage of the community's pulse, extended an invitation for an interview—a parley to decipher the narrative of their undertaking.

"Ms. Martin, Mr. Clark, your efforts have not gone unnoticed," intoned the interviewer, a seasoned journalist with a penchant for unearthing the marrow of the human-interest story. "Pray tell, what spurred this fortification of defenses within the realm of online courtship?"

Sarah, poised before the camera's unblinking gaze, articulated their mission with the eloquence of a seasoned orator. "In the digital age, the pursuit of Eros need not be a labyrinth fraught with Minotaurs," she declared, her words painting the air with gravitas. "We stand as vigilant custodians, ensuring that the path to connection is strewn with the petals of safety rather than the thorns of vulnerability."

Jason, leaning forward with the earnestness of a scholar unveiling a pivotal theorem, added, "Each line of code we inscribe is a testament to our unwavering dedication to the preservation of our users' sanctum. In the hallowed halls of cyberspace, let it be known that we have etched a bastion of trust."

The interview unfolded, a tapestry of discourse and revelation, each thread woven with the dual hues of solemnity and levity. Sarah and Jason elucidated the intricate workings of their security measures, infusing the conversation with anecdotes that sparkled with a wit that belied the gravity of their topic.

As the segment concluded, the anchor turned to the viewers with an appreciative nod. "There you have it, ladies and gentlemen, the architects of amour-propre in the digital domain. Sarah Martin and Jason Clark—guardians of the heart's citadel."

With the cameras dimming, Sarah exchanged a glance with Jason—a silent acknowledgment of the journey they had embarked upon, one that had transformed from a Sisyphean trial into a triumph of collective willpower. They had not merely weathered the storm; they had redirected the winds.

Through the glass facade of the quaint bistro, where Sarah and Jason had convened to toast their recent triumphs, one could observe an ebullient throng, a microcosm of camaraderie and collective exhale after months of digital renovation. The two architects of this newfound security sat at the heart of it all, two pillars of resilience around which trust was being painstakingly rebuilt, brick by cryptographic brick.

"Behold," Sarah proclaimed with a flourish, her voice a melodic overture against the clinking of glasses, "the phoenix rises from the proverbial ashes, not just unscathed but resplendent, its plumage aglow with the sheen of validation."

Jason's chuckle reverberated through the room, a baritone anchor to her soprano sails. "Indeed," he concurred, raising his cup, an elixir of caffeine cradling within like the lifeblood of their countless nocturnal vigils, "the metrics doth not deceive—our digital progeny hath flourished under the vigilant gaze of our collective stewardship."

The screen of Jason's laptop served as a tableau vivant, dynamic graphs and charts illustrating the surge in app downloads and registrations—a visual symphony that crescendo with each new user entrusting their quest for connection to their safeguarded realm. Sarah's gaze drifted toward the window, where the world outside bustled, oblivious to the seismic shift that transpired within the silicon confines of their creation.

"Recall, if you will," she implored the supportive congregation, whose members had become familial in their solidarity, "those halcyon days when our endeavor seemed quixotic, a tilt at the windmills of cyber malfeasance." Her words were tinged with a wistfulness that underscored their shared narrative, one wrought with trials and tribulations that now felt like vestiges of a bygone era.

"Ah, but such quixotry!" Jason interjected, his glasses catching the soft glow of the bistro's ambient lighting, imparting to him the visage of a sage bathed in enlightenment. "For what is valor but the courage to stand fast in the face of adversity, armed with naught but the conviction that the cause is just, and the heart is true?"

Nods of affirmation rippled through the group, each member a testament to the axiom that unity indeed begets strength. They exchanged anecdotes, laughter mingling with introspection, as they dissected every algorithmic conundrum and UX quandary that had been conquered in their collective pursuit of digital sanctuary.

"Let us not forget," Sarah intoned, her eyes alight with the fervor of a general who had led her troops through the fray and emerged victorious, "the fortitude that each of you bestowed upon us. For without your unwavering faith, our fortress might well have crumbled before the first battering ram of doubt struck its gates."

A toast was proposed, the sentiment echoing through the assemblage like a chorus reaching the crescendo of a symphony long in rehearsal. Glasses aloft, they saluted the past, reveled in the present, and dared to peer into the future with a renewed sense of invincibility.

"Here's to the guardianship of hearts," Jason said, the timbre of his voice imbuing the words with a solemn gravity, "and to the indomitable spirit that guides our keystrokes towards a tomorrow replete with promise and devoid of peril."

As the gathering subsided into a harmonious hum of conviviality,
Sarah and Jason shared a glance, a silent accord that bespoke the
depth of their partnership. They had forged more than just a
bastion of safety; they had sculpted a haven, a digital domicile
where single parents could seek serendipity sheltered from the
storm.

Sarah tapped a rhythm on her laptop's edge, the syncopated beat of
a mind already racing towards tomorrow's challenges. Beside her,
Jason scrutinized lines of code that sprawled across his screen like
an intricate tapestry of digital intent, each character woven into
the next with meticulous care.

"Imagine," she mused aloud, drawing a ponderous gaze from Jason,
"a future where our little app becomes the gold standard for online
dating safety."

"Ah, a utopian cyber courtship cosmos," he quipped, pushing his
glasses up the bridge of his nose with a wry smile. "Where single
parents can quest for romance unencumbered by the specter of
trepidation."

"Exactly," Sarah affirmed, her eyes gleaming with the reflection of a
dream taking shape. "And we'll be the architects of that reality.
This is just the inception of our endeavor; there's so much more to
scaffold upon this foundation."

Jason nodded, his own aspirations alight with the sparks of their
shared vision. "We'll weave an ever-tighter web of security
protocols," he said, fingers dancing in the air as if conjuring the
web from thin air. "Each iteration a bulwark against the
machinations of those with malintent."

Her laughter, light and yet laden with the gravitas of their task,
filled the space between them. "You do have a way with words, my
friend. But it's more than just protocols and iterations. It's about
trust—fortifying it, nurturing it. We're building a bastion, yes, but
also a bridge."

"Indeed," he concurred, "a bridge spanning the chasms of doubt, paved with the flagstones of reliability and respect. Our users will cross with their heads held high, knowing that their journey is safeguarded by our relentless vigilance."

"Relentless vigilance," she echoed, savoring the phrase. "But let us not become so ensconced in our cybersecurity citadel that we forget the human element. Our true triumph lies in connections made, families forged, and love's unpredictable voyage across the digital divide."

"Ah, the heart of the matter," Jason said, his expression softening. "For what is a fortress without its inhabitants? Cold stone and echoing corridors. But populate it with hope, laughter, and the occasional shared ice cream sundae, and you have something far stronger than mere walls and towers."

"Shared ice cream sundaes," Sarah repeated, chuckling. "Now that's a security feature I hadn't considered."

"Consider it a metaphorical flavor enhancer," he rejoined with a twinkle in his eye. "After all, even the most fortified castles had their feasts and fables."

"Feasts, fables, and... future plans," she concluded, her voice carrying the weight of responsibility and the lightness of hope in equal measure. "Let's ensure our next chapter is written with the ink of innovation and the parchment of possibilities."

"Then onwards," Jason said, closing his laptop with a gentle click, "to the chronicles of tomorrow. May our code be strong, our intentions pure, and our impact resounding throughout the annals of online amour."

Together, they stood, partners in purpose, guardians of hearts, ready to chart a course through the vast virtual expanse, their resolve as unwavering as the beacon of a lighthouse guiding ships to safe harbor.

Chapter 18

Sarah Martin, ensconced within the comforting embrace of her home office, meticulously scoured the digital underworld for shards of truth that would coalesce into an incontrovertible mosaic of William "Bill" Simmons' past transgressions. With each click, a litany of testimonies from erstwhile partners emerged—each a dolorous echo of betrayal and manipulation. The screen flickered with the ghostly visages of women whose eyes seemed to plead across the binary chasm, their accounts a symphony of sorrow that twined around Sarah's resolve like ivy.

Her fingers danced with precision over keys, compiling records that drew a harrowing portrait of Bill; emails exchanged under the cloak of night, text messages that seethed with latent venom, and scattered police reports that bore witness to a pattern of behavior as unyielding as it was unsettling. Each piece of evidence was a tessera in the mosaic, and Sarah, a modern-day Artemisia of the digital age, wielded her intellect as a chisel, shaping the narrative of justice with unwavering purpose.

"Ah," she murmured to herself, a wry smile touching her lips despite the gravity of her endeavor, "the plot thickens." It was a momentary indulgence in levity, a fragment of dark humor that broke the monolithic seriousness of her task. Her phone—a sleek device that seemed almost sentient in its responsiveness—was now a repository of incriminating exchanges, an arsenal to be deployed at the opportune moment.

Having armored herself with evidence, Sarah turned her attention to the chessboard of human interaction, plotting her next move with the strategic foresight of a grandmaster. She sought a battleground that favored her, a public arena where the watchful eyes of society could serve as both shield and sentinel. It was in the quaint sanctuary of a bustling café, replete with the aroma of roasted coffee beans and the susurrus of hushed conversations, that she would lay her trap.

With the deftness born of necessity, she dispatched a message into the ether, one that would summon Bill to this neutral territory under the guise of pleasantries. Her invitation was couched in civility, yet beneath its surface lurked the steely intent of a woman who had transformed vulnerability into strength. There, amidst the unwitting witnesses of this urban agora, she would confront the enigma that was Bill Simmons, not as prey, but as protagonist in her own odyssey.

In the interstice between planning and execution, Sarah reflected upon the irony of their rendezvous. Here, in the open theatre of the public square, she would peel back the veneer of charm and expose the stygian undercurrents that roiled beneath Bill's placid exterior. It was a curious blend of anticipation and foreboding that settled in her gut, a cognitive dissonance that she quelled with the mantra of preparation and fortitude.

"Checkmate," she whispered to the silent room, a promise not just to herself, but to every shadow that had been cast aside by the likes of Bill. With the stage set and her gambit ready, Sarah Martin steeled herself for the encounter that would redefine the contours of her life.

Sarah stationed herself at a café table, an al fresco bastion of casual surveillance, her eyes scanning for the imminent arrival of Bill Simmons. The marketplace bustled with the cacophony of everyday life, vendors peddling their wares as patrons wove through the maze of commerce with artisan coffees in hand. She had chosen this place for its paradoxical blend of exposure and anonymity, a public square where any altercation would be diluted into the white noise of urban indifference.

Her fingers idly traced the rim of her cup, a gesture of nonchalance belying the adrenal chorus that hummed beneath her skin. As Bill materialized from the throng, his gait exuding an unearned confidence, Sarah straightened with the measured grace of a chess grandmaster poised to advance her queen.

"Bill," she greeted him with a voice that brokered no room for pleasantries, her tone the auditory equivalent of a velvet glove cast over an iron fist. "We need to talk about the skeletons that dance in your closet and how they've been rattling their bones in my direction."

He slid into the chair opposite her, the corners of his mouth twitching upward in a facsimile of charm that failed to reach the frosted tundra of his eyes. "Sarah, darling," he began, his words dripping with condescension like treacle from a spoon, "I'm afraid you're allowing your imagination to run feral. Surely, we can discuss whatever little worries are plaguing your mind."

"Imagination has no dominion here, Bill," she retorted, her resolve an unyielding edifice against the tide of his gaslighting. "This is about reality—the reality of your past transgressions and the way you've tried to ensnare me and my project in your web of deceit."

A flicker of annoyance crossed Bill's features before he recomposed his expression into one of bemused innocence. "You wound me with these baseless accusations," he said, leaning back as if to survey her from a more strategic vantage point. "It seems you've been fed a diet of lies, Sarah. You're seeing phantoms where there's nothing but air."

"Phantoms don't leave traces, Bill." Her words were a rapier thrust, precise and unflinching. "But manipulators, abusers—they leave patterns, evidence. And I'm not the only one who's seen the pattern of your behavior."

Bill's jaw tightened, the veneer of affability beginning to crack as the realization dawned upon him that Sarah was no mere damsel in distress; she was a formidable opponent, armed with truth and undaunted by his denials. His smile faltered; the act unsustainable when faced with the unwavering gaze of a woman who had come to reclaim her power.

"Your conviction is misplaced," he said after a moment, a note of warning threading through his rebuttal. "And it would be in your best interest to reconsider the path you're heading down."

"Consideration is the purview of the thoughtful, Bill," she replied, her composure a steel- clad testament to her determination. "And I have considered every piece of the puzzle you've unwittingly laid out for me. The picture is clear, and it's not one I'll allow to be hung on my wall."

With that, Sarah watched as Bill wrestled with the dawning comprehension that his usual ploys were rendered impotent in the face of her relentless pursuit of justice. It was a battle of wills where she had already mapped the terrain, calculated the risks, and emerged ready to stand her ground.

Sarah unfurled a sheaf of papers across the café table, her fingers unhesitating as they traced the line graphs and pie charts of evidence—a cartographer charting the topography of deceit. Each document bore the weight of truth, culminating in an irrefutable composite of Bill's past transgressions. Screenshots, their edges crinkling under the tension of her touch, gleamed with the incandescent glow of exposed lies; messages, once cloaked in the guise of affection, now stood stark against the barren landscape of manipulation.

"Here," she said, her voice imbued with the gravitas of a judge delivering a verdict, "are the testimonies—narratives that weave a tapestry so intricate it would be folly to dismiss them as mere fabrications."

Bill's countenance, previously a mask of controlled nonchalance, contorted into a tableau of defense and indignation. His lips curled back over words that sought to rebuke the assault on his character, but they landed with the impotence of arrows against a bastion. The fortress of his self-assuredness had been besieged by undeniable proof, each piece a cannonade against the ramparts of his denial.

"Surely you see that these are the machinations of the jealous, the vindictive," he seethed, the timbre of his voice strained as taut as the strings of a violin, wailing under the bow of Sarah's resolve. "You're not immune to the contagion of spite that has clearly infected these... these people."

Sarah's eyebrow arched, the gesture a silent sonnet of skepticism. She watched him squirm, an intellectual voyeur to the unraveling of a man whose arsenal of gaslight and guile suddenly seemed as antiquated as a flintlock pistol in the age of digital warfare.

"Jealousy is a curious lens through which to view accountability," she retorted. Her words were articulated pieces of armor encasing her stance, a panoply of reason and righteousness. "And spite, I assure you, is not the currency in which I trade."

Bill's anger burgeoned like a storm cloud on the horizon, dark and brooding. Yet Sarah remained the lighthouse steadfast on the rock, her beacon of evidence a guide for any who might navigate the treacherous waters he had churned. The public's eyes began to alight upon the scene, drawn by the gravity of confrontation, sensing the seismic shift beneath the veneer of everyday café pleasantries.

"Your claims," Bill spat, "are as hollow as the echo chamber from which they've undoubtedly emerged."

"Then consider this chamber a concert hall," Sarah replied, the allegro of her wit undiminished, "and my claims the symphony that will herald your denouement."

Bill's jaw tightened, a visual testament to the crescendo of ire that bloomed within him, its roots entangling any semblance of restraint he may have harbored. Sarah witnessed this transformation with the detached curiosity of a scholar observing an experiment's inevitable reaction, her own equilibrium unshaken by the acidic spittle of aggression that now flecked his speech.

"Your little digital crusade," he began, the words tinged with a venomous mirth that failed to reach the cold hearth of his eyes,

"It's a house of cards, Sarah. And I—I am the tempest that could huff and puff and send it all tumbling down."

The threat, veiled in the nursery rhymes of menace, was as palpable as the tension that thrummed in the air between them. Yet Sarah's response was not one of fear but rather the serene clarity of one who has navigated far stormier seas. Her voice remained as steady as a metronome amid an orchestra's crescendo, each word a note played in perfect tempo.

"Tempests," she replied, the corner of her mouth curving with a wryness that belied the gravity of his intimidation, "have a way of revealing the true integrity of what they assail. A well-built fortress stands, a flimsy facade falls away."

She leaned forward infinitesimally, the motion deliberates, an embodiment of her unwavering resolve. The evidence she had meticulously compiled was an anchor, holding her steadfast in the choppy waters of Bill's burgeoning rage. It was not just a defense but a declaration, an assertion that her cause was just, her actions warranted, and her spirit indomitable.

"Go ahead," she continued, her gaze locking with his in a silent challenge that resonated with the certainty of a bell struck in a silent chamber, "unleash your storm, Bill. But remember, when the winds you've summoned howl and scream, it is your own foundation you risk eroding."

Bill's hands formed fists upon the table, the white of his knuckles a stark contrast against the wood grain, a physical manifestation of the turmoil that roiled within him. His threats were the last refuge of a man cornered by his own misdeeds, a desperate ploy to regain some semblance of control where there was none to be had.

Sarah, however, did not so much as flinch at the display of fury. She understood that the measure of one's character lay in the ability to face adversity without losing oneself to it. And in this moment, beneath the watchful eyes of an unwitting audience, she was the embodiment of poise under pressure, a testament to the strength that lies in standing one's ground, even as the gale forces of another's wrath seek to uproot and destabilize.

"Nevertheless," Sarah pronounced, the word cutting through the ambient clamor of the bustling café like a surgeon's scalpel, precise and unerringly steady, "I find myself compelled to iterate, Bill, that the universe has an uncanny knack for maintaining its ledger, a meticulous bookkeeper tallying the moral debits and credits of our actions." The corner of her lip curled upwards in a wry smile, not touching the determined glint in her eyes.

Bill's posture stiffened, his face a mask of indignation struggling against the revelation of vulnerability beneath. He seemed to shrink, fractionally, as if each syllable she spoke chipped away at the edifice he presented to the world.

"Your machinations," she continued, unfazed by his simmering rage, "are but gossamer threads in the grand tapestry of consequence, easily rendered by the merest flicker of truth." Her fingers splayed across the dossier of evidence before her, a tactile reminder of the potency contained within its pages.

The ebb and flow of the café's patrons slowed; their collective attention snagged by the gravity of the discourse unfolding before them. Whispers coalesced into murmurs, heads turned, and curious eyes peered over steaming mugs of coffee, drawn inexorably towards the drama at the center of their unassuming refuge from the quotidian.

"Consider this your clarion call to penance," Sarah intoned, her voice the embodiment of equanimity, even as Bill's visage contorted with the frustration of a man watching his fortress besieged, "for the repercussions of your deeds are as relentless as the tide, and just as unforgiving."

The audience, now fully captivated, bore witness to the spectacle, a living tableau vivant of accountability in action. They were the Greek chorus to this modern tragedy, where hubris was met not with nemesis, but with the inexorable force of a woman undeterred by intimidation or deceit.

Sarah's voice, a steadfast beacon amidst the cacophony of half-heard conversations and clinking porcelain, rose in steady cadence. Her words, though spoken with the precision of a scalpel's edge, were not merely cut—they carved, sculpted from the air itself a monument to resilience that those gathered could not help but admire. As she articulated the litany of grievances, her resolve kindled a fire in the hearts of those who had once cowered in the shadow of Bill's duplicity.

From the periphery of confrontation, a woman stepped forward, emboldened by Sarah's unwavering stance. With a timbre rich in both vulnerability and valor, she added her own testament to the pyre of evidence. "I, too, have danced with this devil," she confessed, her gaze locked onto Bill's faltering countenance, "and bore the leaden weight of his false promises upon my shoulders." Her declaration, a domino, set forth a cascade; others emerged from the throng, each narrative a thread weaving into the ever-expanding tapestry of truth.

Bill's visage, once an enigmatic mask of charm and guile, now betrayed the fracturing of his composure under public scrutiny. The color drained from his face as if the gravity of his exposed sins was leeching his very essence. His lips parted in feeble protest, the words stumbling out like marionettes dispossessed of their strings—awkward, unconvincing, and, impotent against the mounting chorus of voices rising against him.

"Your artifice," Sarah declared, her eyes two smoldering coals of conviction, "is as ephemeral as morning mist before the blaze of the sun's scrutiny." Each syllable punctuated the air, a staccato rhythm that seemed to resonate with the very heartbeat of the gathering crowd. Bill's attempts at defense became a spectacle, a tragicomic display of a man grasping at straws while the swift river of consequence eroded the ground beneath him.

The murmurs among the onlookers swelled into a tide of righteous indignation, washing over the scene with palpable force. Bill, now a figure diminished and isolated, stood encircled not just by those he had wronged, but by the collective judgment of society itself. It was a crucible from which there would be no emergence unscathed, a reckoning wrought by the hands of the once-silenced, now given voice through Sarah's unyielding fortitude.

Sarah, undeterred by the tempest she had conjured, remained the eye of the storm—a paragon of composed defiance that not only confronted but dismantled the facade of a man who had built his world on deception's fragile foundation.

The viral conflagration of Sarah's revelation, once kindled by the flint and steel of her indomitable will, spread with the ferocity of a bushfire in a parched savanna, scorching the lush facade that Bill had so meticulously cultivated. As word of his nefarious past tore through the digital ether, it left in its wake a smoldering path of ruin, tarnishing the sheen of his reputation with the indelible soot of truth. The very air seemed to crackle with the electricity of collective epiphany, as screens across the city flickered with the visage of a man unmasked.

Coursing through social media veins, the narrative of his misdeeds became a rallying cry for the silenced, a beacon that drew forth from the shadows those too long cowed by the specter of repercussion. Screenshots, once imprisoned behind the fear-forged bars of private galleries, leapt forth into the public domain, each pixelated glyph a testament to the pattern of predation that had been Bill's modus operandi. There was no corner of cyberspace unlit by the lurid glow of his exposure, no algorithmic crevice where his name did not resonate with the sibilant hiss of societal scorn.

Meanwhile, the erstwhile puppeteer of hearts found himself bereft of strings to pull; his manipulative machinations laid bare as the hollow stratagems they were. The law, that slumbering Leviathan, stirred from its inertia, roused by the clamor for justice that rang out with the clarity of a clarion call. The constabulary machinery ground into motion, its gears lubricated by the oil of public outcry, as the full weight of legal consequence began to inexorably press down upon Bill's shoulders.

He stood, a figure at once pitiable and reviled, as the social edifice he had erected crumbled about him. Each withdrawal of support, each renunciation by former allies and fair-weather friends, was a brick pulled from the foundation of his feigned respectability. And as the structure of his deception imploded, so did the illusion of his unassailability, leaving him exposed to the elements of accountability that swept in to fill the void.

His previous aura of enigma, which had lent him an almost magnetic allure, now curdled into an odious miasma of infamy. It clung to him, a spectral shroud that marked him as one who had gambled with the trust of others and lost spectacularly against the house of human decency. In the court of public opinion, the gavel fell with resounding finality, sentencing him to a purgatory of ostracism from which there would be no reprieve.

In this grand theater of consequence, Sarah watched from the wings, her role as the architect of revelation complete. Her countenance, once etched with the lines of wary circumspection, now bore the faintest trace of a wry smile—a silent acknowledgment of the irony that Bill, in his hubris, had become ensnared by the very web of deceit he had woven. The serious humor of the universe seldom revealed itself so plainly, but when it did, it was as incisive as it was poetic.

And thus, the stage was set for the denouement of William "Bill" Simmons, as the curtain descended on his reign of manipulation, the audience of society having rendered its irrevocable verdict.

Sarah Martin, her silhouette sharpened by the cathartic fires of a battle fought and won, stood before the app's interface with an air of solemnity. Her fingers, once hesitant as they danced across the screen in search of connection, now moved with the surety of a maestro conducting a symphony of renewal. With each keystroke, she orchestrated a suite of new features, security protocols singing into existence to safeguard the digital terrain where hearts sought solace and kinship.

Her eyes, those twin sentinels that had watched over the tumultuous journey from its inception, gleamed with the unassailable light of one who has traversed the abyss and emerged not just unscathed, but emboldened. Here was Sarah Martin, a cartographer charting the terra incognita of single parents' vulnerability within the online dating cosmos, transforming it into a bastion of assured sanctuary.

Indeed, it was as though the app itself had become an extension of her own indomitable spirit—a citadel of safety forged from the crucible of her resolve. It bore the imprimatur of her experience, each line of code infused with her ethos, an unwavering commitment to the protection of those who, like her, sought a second chapter amidst the annals of love and companionship.

Within this sanctified space, Sarah stood as both sentinel and sage, her narrative no longer confined to the margins of victimhood but elevated to the annals of valiance. The tapestry of her life, interwoven with threads of tenacity and grace, now served as a standard for others to rally beneath—a beacon signaling the dawn of a new epoch in which the ghosts of predation would find no quarter.

As the digital landscape flourished under her stewardship, so did the chorus of voices uplifted by her courage. They came forth in a crescendo of support, resonating through the very framework of society, extolling the virtues of a woman who, with wit and wisdom, had redrawn the boundaries of what it meant to seek love in the age of pixels and profiles.

In the grand narrative of Sarah Martin's life, a new chapter burgeoned forth from the pages—a testament to the power of resilience and the alchemy of self-reclamation. Her story, etched into the annals of the digital age, stood as a palimpsest of hope for all who navigated the serpentine pathways of the heart's desires. And therein lay the beauty of her triumph: not in the silence of a foe vanquished, but in the symphony of lives empowered, echoing endlessly into the vast expanse of human connection.

Chapter 19

Sarah, her fingers tapping a staccato rhythm against the glass surface of her smartphone, perused through the digital mosaic of potential love interests that populated the dating app with the discernment of a curator selecting art for an exclusive exhibition. Ensconced in the corner of a chic café, she sipped her latte as if it were an elixir of fortitude, steeling herself for another incursion into the fray of online courtship. The profiles swiped left carried the visages and promises of connections not meant to be; those swiped right bore the possibility of kindred spirits—fellow single parents who understood the intricate ballet of balancing affection for one's offspring with the pursuit of romantic fulfillment.

Amidst this ritual, Sarah's mind was unyieldingly tethered to the paramountcy of her child's well-being, transforming each prospective match into a question—a riddle composed of background checks and subtle interrogations camouflaged within casual conversation. Her successful career had honed her intuition for people's intentions, yet the digital realm demanded a hyper-vigilance that bridled her natural ebullience.

Later that evening, amidst the sanctuary of her support group, Sarah recounted the tales of her digital paramours with an air of levity that belied the gravity of her quest. The room, a tableau of earnest faces bathed in the warm glow of sympathetic understanding, became her sounding board. She spoke of the suitor who boasted a rapier wit but displayed a gallery of trophy-hunting photos that clashed with her own ethos, and of the gentle soul whose narrative of resilience mirrored her own journey, yet geographical chasms lay between them.

"Online dating is akin to navigating a labyrinth designed by Escher," she quipped, "full of steps leading to uncertain destinations and perspectives that shift just when you think you've found a clear path." Her companions chuckled at the simile, recognizing the blend of humor and depth that characterized

Sarah's approach to life's conundrums.

As she solicited counsel from her peers, Sarah's articulation of her encounters oscillated between self-deprecating anecdotes and astute analyses, revealing both vulnerability and an indomitable spirit in her search for companionship. It was a delicate dance of sharing experiences without relinquishing too much control, seeking guidance while maintaining the helm of her ship, navigating through personal storms and doldrums with an eye ever fixed on the horizon where heart and safety lay in harmonious coexistence.

Sarah scrolled through the forum, her fingers pausing as she contemplated her next words. Around her, the support group formed a semi-circle of solidarity, laptops aglow, each member immersed in the collective endeavor to distill their online dating sagas into cautionary yet enlightening tales for the digital ether.

"Consider the parable of the chameleon," mused Michael, his eyes reflecting the wisdom of one who had weathered many a romantic squall, "a creature adept at changing its skin, yet beneath those shifting colors lurks an unchanging essence. So too must we be wary of those who mask their true selves behind the seductive veneer of a profile."

Rebecca, ever the reticent scribe, typed with tentative strokes, translating her trepidation into a narrative that resonated with the silent fears of countless others. "It's about unraveling the tapestry of half-truths," she whispered, as though confiding in the keys themselves, "to find the strands of sincerity woven within."

Emily, whose laughter often served as the group's clarion call back to hope, shared an anecdote of whimsy wrapped in prudence. "I encountered a modern-day Odysseus, regaling me with tales of adventures and close encounters. Yet, for all his wanderlust, it was I who journeyed back to Ithaca alone, armed only with the knowledge that not all who roam are lost, but some are best left to their odyssey."

Their collected experiences unfurled across the screen, a mosaic of memoirs and musings that took shape under Sarah's orchestration, her deft keystrokes weaving the threads of their individual stories into a cohesive chronicle. It was a digital quilt, offering warmth and warning in equal measure to those who sought solace from the cold uncertainties of seeking connection in a world reduced to swipes and pixels.

"Let us broadcast our experiences into the vast expanse of cyberspace," declared Sarah, her voice a beacon cutting through the fog of apprehension that so often shrouded the pursuit of affection, "not as scaremongers perched upon soapboxes of self-righteousness, but as cartographers charting the treacherous waters of the heart, that others may sail more safely."

Together, they crafted posts that were candid and clever, erudite yet accessible, their collective intellect shining through in the prose that danced with humor despite the gravity of its message. They were not just participants in the online forums but vigilant guardians, standing watch over the virtual realms where hearts ventured in search of kinship.

As the session ended, the hum of computers hushed, and the members leaned back, regarding each other with a sense of accomplishment interlaced with camaraderie. They had laid bare their vulnerabilities, spun them into wisdom, and dispatched it across the digital divide, where it would serve as both lighthouse and life raft for those navigating the capricious seas of online dating.

Sarah, the perennial beacon of prudence in a world brimming with digital dalliances, took to the podium amidst a sea of attentive faces, her countenance exuding a confidence that belied the tumult of her journey. The auditorium, a cavernous vessel for the convergence of single parents seeking camaraderie and counsel, echoed with the palpable anticipation of shared narratives. It was here, under the unforgiving fluorescence, that Sarah and her co-crusaders, Rebecca, Michael, and Emily, embarked upon the oratorical odyssey of imparting wisdom gleaned from their own amorous escapades within the pixelated plains of romance.

"Let us navigate these uncharted territories with the tenacity of seasoned explorers," Sarah intoned, her voice a harmonious blend of authority and empathy, suffused with a gentle mirth that disarmed even the most guarded of hearts. "For we are not merely seekers of love's sweet embrace, but custodians of the tender sanctity that is our children's well- being."

Rebecca offered anecdotes as vibrant tapestries woven from threads of caution and triumph, her words painting portraits of resilience. Michael, in his characteristic sagacity, dissected the anatomy of conversation, advising on the discernment between genuine connection and deceptive charm. Emily, with an alacrity almost prophetic, demystified the enigmatic algorithms that dictated the ebb and flow of matches, her insights illuminating the path to judicious engagement.

The audience, a congregation bound by a common yearning, absorbed each syllable, their nodding heads and scribbling pens attesting to the value of the counsel bestowed upon them. Laughter, that universal salve, punctuated the proceedings, as the speakers masterfully interspersed their sagacious discourse with quips that reflected a truth universally acknowledged: in the pursuit of love, one must retain a sense of humor lest they succumb to despair.

As the evening waned, Sarah felt a burgeoning resolve crystallize within her. She envisioned the contours of a literary endeavor, one that would encapsulate the odyssey of her heart—a compendium of cautionary tales, pragmatic strategies, and the indefatigable hope that propelled her forward. Her experiences, once confined to the ephemeral exchanges of support groups and online forums, now yearned for permanence within the pages of a tome.

"Friends, I stand before you, an acolyte of affection, armed with little more than my chronicles and the fervent desire to illuminate the shadows that lurk within the realm of virtual courtship," she proclaimed, her declaration reverberating through the assembly. "I shall embark upon this literary quest, to catalog our collective sojourns into the maelstrom of matchmaking, that our progeny may venture forth with foresight and fortitude."

And thus, with the inkling of her first sentence already etching itself upon the canvas of her mind, Sarah resolved to write a book—a beacon of guidance for fellow navigators of love's labyrinthine landscape, a testament to the indomitable spirit of single parents adrift in the cybernetic quest for companionship, all while steadfastly anchoring their sails to the safe harbors of their offspring's security.

Sarah Martin, perched on the precipice of her ergonomic chair, fingers cavorting across the keyboard with a finesse befitting a seasoned pianist, found herself immersed in the collaborative alchemy of transforming raw, often harrowing personal narratives into didactic prose. The gentle glow of her computer screen bathed her face in a soft luminescence as she and her cohorts poured over the drafts of their impending articles for various esteemed publications, each keystroke a deliberate effort to distill the essence of their collective wisdom.

"Consider this," she mused aloud, her voice a melodic timbre that belied the gravity of her words. "We are not merely scribing words; we are weaving a tapestry of cautionary anecdotes and sagacious counsel, designed to safeguard the unsuspecting heart from the potential quicksand hidden amidst the digital flora of courtship."

Rebecca, Michael, and Emily, her compatriots in this noble endeavor, nodded in solemn agreement, their gazes fixed upon their respective screens as they navigated the treacherous waters of syntax and semantics. It was akin to a modern-day symposium, where the Socratic method had been supplanted by backspaces and cursor blinks, and the pursuit of Eros demanded vigilance against the specter of deceit.

"Let us embellish our discourse with humor," Sarah proposed, her countenance alight with a mischievous sparkle. "For it is through the amalgamation of levity and learning that we may most effectively inoculate our readers against the maladies of misplaced trust."

They shared a collective chuckle, understanding that even in the quagmire of online dating's pitfalls, there was room for wit to act as a balm for the soul's bruises. Thus, their writing took on a dual nature, at once both erudite and whimsically self-deprecating, a veritable confluence of scholarly jest and earnest admonition.

With the articles dispatched to their editorial destinations, Sarah turned her attention to the vast expanse of social media, that omnipresent coliseum where opinions clashed and experiences were disseminated with the abandon of autumn leaves in a tempest. Here, in the domain of tweets and status updates, she and her band of intrepid single parents would engage in a different kind of dialectic, one punctuated by hashtags and infused with the immediacy of lived experience.

"Behold the double-edged sword of technological intimacy," she proclaimed, crafting a post with the meticulous care of a sculptor chiseling away at marble. "Herein lies the paradox: the very tools that connect us also harbor the capacity to rend asunder."

Her followers, accustomed now to Sarah's blend of intellectual musings and candid revelations, engaged with her posts with fervor, sharing their own stories in a cascade of solidarity. The support group's presence burgeoned, their digital footprints leaving indelible marks upon the consciousness of an audience ever-thirsty for authenticity.

As Sarah watched the comments proliferate like a verdant vine reaching toward the sun, she allowed herself a moment of satisfaction. This was more than mere dissemination of information; it was the germination of a community, bound together by the common threads of longing and prudence. With each shared article, each crafted tweet, they were not only illuminating the potential dangers lurking behind amorous avatars but also fostering a haven where the heart could seek its match, tempered by the wisdom of those who had traversed the terrain before.

Sarah Martin, surveying the modest assembly of single parents gathered within the confines of the local community center's linoleum-floored hall, couldn't help but let the ghost of a smile play at the corners of her mouth. The air was thick with anticipation and a hint of cafeteria coffee as she prepared to inaugurate the first in a series of workshops designed to shepherd the unwary through the labyrinthine world of online dating, a domain as rife with potential as it was fraught with peril.

"Welcome, intrepid navigators of the heart's unpredictable seas," she began, her voice imbued with the gravitas of experience yet underpinned by a timbre of camaraderie. "Today, we embark upon a journey not just of romantic discovery, but of tactical enlightenment."

The group, an eclectic coterie of hopeful romantics clad in attire that ranged from business casual to 'just managed to get the kids to school', leaned in, their expressions a mosaic of earnestness and trepidation. Sarah unveiled a PowerPoint presentation, each slide a meticulous amalgam of statistics, personal anecdotes, and bullet-pointed strategies for vetting prospective matches with the thoroughness of a seasoned detective.

"Let us not be cavalier with our hearts, nor with the safety of our progeny," she advised, clicking to a slide festooned with the iconography of red flags. "For in this digital bazaar of affection, not every merchant deals in sincerity."

Nods punctuated her declaration as if they were rhythmic affirmations, each attendee mentally arming themselves with the wisdom imparted. Amidst the chorus of agreement, Rebecca, known for her penchant for over-preparation, jotted notes with the fervor of a scribe capturing sacred scripture, while Michael, whose humor served as his shield, quipped sotto voce about crafting an algorithm to filter out the undesirables, eliciting a ripple of chuckles that momentarily lifted the seminar's earnest veneer.

Meanwhile, in collaboration with the stalwarts of academia and the sentinels of youth development, Sarah and her compatriots shaped a curriculum destined for the hallowed halls of education: a program tailored to inoculate young adults against the seductive illusions often peddled on the highways and byways of cyberspace. In partnership with teachers and community leaders, they crafted lesson plans that interwove the threads of caution with the yarns of optimism, knitting together a tapestry of guidance that would arm the uninitiated with the armor of informed decision-making.

"Consider this," Sarah posited during a symposium held in the echoic auditorium of the local high school, "that to arm oneself with knowledge is to transform vulnerability into empowerment." Her voice resonated, not merely off the walls, but within the minds of those assembled, a motley crew of adolescents teetering on the precipice of adulthood, their smartphones clutched like talismans against the ambiguity of growing up.

"Your courtship with technology need not be a dance with danger," she continued, her words a potent cocktail of erudition and colloquialism, "provided you step to the rhythm of prudence and keep your wits about you as steadfast partners."

As the workshop attendees dispersed, and the students filed out of the auditorium, the seedlings of awareness took root within the fertile soil of their comprehension. Sarah watched them go, her heart buoyant with the weightless joy of one who has charted a course through troubled waters and now lights beacons for others to follow. She knew the perils of love in the age of algorithms all too well, but with each seminar, each educational endeavor, she was rewriting the narrative—one keystroke, one heart-to-heart at a time.

Sarah perched at the edge of a plush armchair, the studio lights casting an ethereal glow upon her countenance as she prepared to unravel the skein of her online dating odyssey. The camera lens trained on her with unblinking scrutiny, a Cyclops seeking truths from the depths of human experience. Flanked by Rebecca, Michael, and Emily, comrades-in-arms in this crusade for cautionary courtship tales, Sarah cleared her throat, a prelude to the symphony of shared wisdom about to be broadcast.

"Online dating," she began, her timbre rich with conviction, "is akin to navigating a vast ocean with both treasure and treachery lurking beneath its surface. It behooves us, therefore, to chart our course with judicious care." Her colleagues nodded, a silent chorus of assent to the gravity and levity of their collective message.

As the interview progressed, the support group wove a tapestry of personal vignettes, punctuated by laughter that belied deeper currents of resilience. Their anecdotes served dual purposes: illuminating the shadowy corners of virtual romance and kindling sparks of camaraderie amongst those who had trodden similar paths.

"Always meet in public," quipped Michael, his eyes twinkling with mirth behind spectacles that had slipped down the bridge of his nose, "lest your date turn out to have a personality as appealing as a dial-up connection."

"Indeed," chimed in Rebecca, "your suitor's charming emoticons might belie the fact that their only long-term relationship is with their parole officer."

The segment concluded with earnest entreaties to listeners, urging vigilance without veering into the territory of fear. As the red recording light dimmed, Sarah felt a surge of gratification, knowing that their collective voice would ripple through airwaves and fiber-optic cables, reaching countless unseen others.

In the days that followed, feedback poured in like a salve for the soul. Emails and messages brimmed with gratitude, telling tales of dodged bullets and newfound prudence in the digital realms of romance. Each note bolstered Sarah's resolve, fueling her mission with fresh purpose.

"Your story stopped me from ignoring the red flags," wrote one relieved dater, whose brush with peril had been averted by heeding Sarah's counsel.

"Your advice was a lighthouse in my fog of loneliness," another confessed, finding safe harbor in the strategies shared by the group.

With each testimonial, Sarah and her cohort solidified their role as sentinels of the heart's safety, a band of merry mentors guiding love's seekers through the labyrinthine web of modern matchmaking. Their jests and judicious tips had become beacons, and the feedback a clarion call to continue their voyage across the airwaves and beyond, heralding the gospel of guarded hearts in a world where love could be but a swipe away.

Chapter 20

Sarah, always the epitome of prudence, sat before her laptop's luminescent glow, eyes flickering with a mix of skepticism and latent optimism. The rhythmic tapping of her fingers against the keyboard punctuated the silence of her meticulously organized home office, a testament to her unwavering commitment to both her career and her role as a vigilant single mother. She navigated the dating app with an analytical mind, each swipe a calculated assessment of potential risks and rewards.

The men who paraded across her screen were a motley assortment of hopeful bachelors, each presenting a facade curated for digital appeal. Sarah entertained these virtual courtships with the precision of a chess master, ensuring that every rendezvous was meticulously planned within the public sphere, her well-being and that of her child, paramount above the whimsical quest for companionship. It was a delicate dance of introspection and outward observation, where coffee shops became arenas of character judgment, and casual conversation, a sieve for intentions.

Amidst this carousel of cautious encounters, a singular profile emerged from the sea of possibilities, arresting Sarah's astute gaze. Mark's digital representation bore an air of authenticity that pierced through the commonplace braggadocio often flaunted online. His smile radiated sincerity; his words, devoid of the usual pretense, seemed to echo Sarah's own thoughts with uncanny resonance. They shared a lexicon of interests, from the literary classics to the simple joy found in nature's embrace, crafting a tapestry of mutual understanding with each exchanged message.

As their dialogue unfolded, the text on the screen transformed into a conduit for genuine connection, a rarity in the ephemeral world of online dalliances. Their conversations meandered through existential musings and playful banter, weaving the initial threads of affinity into a fabric robust enough to warrant the leap from pixels to palpable reality. It was as though fate had conspired to align two stars in the vast firmament of the internet—a cosmic jest at the expense of probability.

And so, Sarah, ever the sentinel of her own heart, permitted herself a morsel of hope, allowing the notion of Mark to germinate in the fertile soil of her contemplation. Amidst the jocular quips they exchanged, there lay a profound undercurrent of possibility, a chance that her meticulous curation of suitors might have serendipitously led her to someone worthy of the sacred enclave she had built around her life and the life of her child.

Sarah stepped into the café, her senses immediately inundated by the aromatic amalgam of roasted coffee beans and freshly baked pastries—a sensory sonnet that played harmoniously with the anticipation thrumming in her veins. She scanned the cozy interior, eyes alighting upon a man whose presence commanded the space around him, not through ostentation but with an unspoken confidence that was as inviting as the warm ambiance of the establishment itself. This was Mark.

They greeted with a handshake that morphed seamlessly into a congenial embrace, the kind of touch that whispered promises of comfort without overstepping the boundaries of newfound acquaintance. As they settled into the cushioned intimacy of the corner booth, the timbre of their voices melded with the soft cadence of acoustic melodies serenading the room, creating a private symphony that underscored their dialogue.

With every word exchanged, Sarah found herself ensconced in a tapestry of delightful conversation that was both erudite and effervescent. Mark's humor was a subtle brew, a deft blend of wit and self-deprecation that never failed to elicit from Sarah a cascade of genuine laughter—a sound she realized had been a scarce resident in the halls of her recent history.

"Life," Mark mused, his gaze holding hers with an earnestness that belied the lightness of his tone, "is rather like a cup of coffee, don't you think? Each sip a moment to savor, each drop a narrative unto itself, yet it is only in taking our time to appreciate the full cup that we truly relish the experience."

"Indeed," Sarah replied, the corners of her mouth curving upward in amusement. "And just like coffee, relationships are best when not rushed. The slow brew often yields the richest flavor." Her voice held a lilt of playfulness, yet the depth of her conviction resonated clear and true.

As their encounter meandered through the landscapes of casual revelations and shared aspirations, Sarah found herself enveloped in a sense of ease that she hadn't realized she'd been yearning for. Mark's attentiveness was a gentle tide, lapping at the shores of her reticence without ever threatening to flood her defenses. He listened with a focus that made her feel seen—truly seen—and not merely as a silhouette against the canvas of single parenthood.

In the days that followed, the bond between them burgeoned with each shared experience, each act of mutual understanding. Mark navigated the delicate balance of Sarah's life with the finesse of a maestro conducting a symphony of intricate harmonies. He recognized the gravity of her role as a mother, and rather than vying for the limelight, he offered support like a steady undercurrent, empowering her to shine in her multifaceted roles.

"Your strength," Mark confided during a stroll through the dappled shade of the park, "is not diminished by the weight of your responsibilities, but rather augmented by the grace with which you bear them." His words were not flattery but a mirror reflecting the reality of her resilience—a trait Sarah had learned to wield with aplomb but seldom had acknowledged by another.

It was this profound respect, this quiet reinforcement of her boundaries, that coaxed the tendrils of trust from the protective shell Sarah had constructed. Mark did not rush her; he walked beside her, step by patient step, on a path they were paving together—one built on the foundation of mutual respect and the shared belief that the best things in life are those worth waiting for.

Sarah slid the last of the folding chairs into a neat row, turning to offer a reassuring smile as Mark entered the room, his presence an amiable beacon amid the thrum of eager chatter from her support group. The motley assembly of single parents, each a veteran of life's unpredictable tides, paused in their conversations to appraise the newcomer with a collective curiosity typically reserved for rare specimens under a microscope.

"Everyone," Sarah's voice, tinged with a quiet pride, beckoned their attention, "this is Mark."

A palpable hum of approval rose from the group as Mark extended his hand, not with the ostentatious flourish of a peacock fanning its feathers, but with the unassuming grace of a man well-versed in the vernacular of genuine human connection. His handshake was neither a limp fish nor a vice grip but struck that delicate balance indicative of equanimity and warmth.

As anecdotes and laughter ricocheted around the room, it became abundantly clear that Mark, much like a seasoned gardener who understands that the true essence of growth lies not solely in the sunlight but also in the nurturing soil, had effortlessly sown seeds of camaraderie amongst the once-guarded hearts. He listened intently to tales of temper tantrums and teenage tribulations, offering nods, and knowing smiles that served as silent sonnets to the shared struggles of their singular parenting odyssey.

Later, as Sarah and Mark indulged in the pursuit of new experiences, they traversed the landscape of local museums, their voices low and harmonious, weaving through exhibits like two solitary streams converging into a confluence of mutual understanding. Each painting, each sculpture, stood testament to the fact that art, much like their burgeoning relationship, was a dialogue—a conversation between creator and beholder, each bringing their own narrative to the communion.

It was during a pottery class, hands cloaked in the cool, wet clay, that their laughter erupted with the unbridled joy of children discovering the magic of mud pies for the first time. As the wheel spun, their fingers danced in a duet of creation and mirth, crafting not just misshapen vessels destined for the anonymity of a cupboard, but memories etched with the indelible ink of shared endeavor.

Through each excursion, each carefully curated date, Mark and Sarah found solace in the solidarity of their circumstances. They reveled in the discovery of shared passions and the comfort of silent understandings, their camaraderie blossoming like a night-blooming cereus—rare, beautiful, and even more precious for its ephemeral nature.

In the tapestry of their encounters, woven with threads of humor and the rich hues of empathy, it was evident that they were not merely two souls seeking solace in companionship but architects of a sanctuary where the trials of single parenthood were met not with trepidation but with resilient joie de vivre. Together, they navigated the labyrinthine journey of finding love anew, each step forward a testament to the belief that the heart, no matter how cautious, possesses an infinite capacity for renewal amidst life's intricate dance.

The evening's quietude encased Sarah's abode, a sanctum of solitude where thoughts could perambulate unfettered by the day's clamor. As she reclined upon her chaise, an oasis amidst the orderly chaos that was the hallmark of a single mother's dwelling, Sarah's gaze fell upon her phone—an unassuming conduit to realms erstwhile uncharted. Her fingers skated across its screen with a deftness born of habit, tracing the digital breadcrumbs of her recent forays into the world of online dating.

It was a peculiar odyssey, fraught with the specter of unknown intentions and the inherent risks of virtual courtship; yet it burgeoned with the promise of connectivity, the potential to intertwine lonesome orbits. The app had been her compass, guiding her through the murky waters of new beginnings with the steadiness of its safety features—a lighthouse beckoning her towards havens of like-minded souls. And there, amid the flotsam of tentative greetings and fleeting conversations, she had discovered Mark—a kindred spirit whose genuineness shimmered like a beacon in the shallow tide pools of superficial exchanges.

In this reflective repose, Sarah pondered the duality of her experiences—how each swipe, each typed disclosure, was a gamble against the odds of disingenuousness. Yet, therein lay the splendor of human endeavor: to risk the known for the allure of what might be. It was a delicate ballet of trust and caution, each step measured, each twirl scrutinized under the watchful eye of prudence. She had learned to listen not just with her ears but with the intuition honed by motherhood and past heartaches, discerning truth from pretense with the precision of a maestro orchestrating a symphony of sincerity.

Her musings were interrupted by a cascade of notifications, testimonials from fellow voyagers in the realm of affectionate pursuit. Each ping was an affirmation, a chorus heralding success stories that wove themselves into the fabric of the app's burgeoning legacy. Single parents, once ensconced within their own citadels of routine, now shared vignettes of happiness found and loneliness vanquished, bolstering the app's repute as a bastion of hopeful hearts.

With a smile tugging at the corners of her lips, Sarah recognized the reciprocity of her journey—that by venturing forth, she had become both beacon and beneficiary in this collective cartography of connection. In her quest, she had not only found Mark but inadvertently sown seeds of courage in others, emboldening them to navigate the tempestuous seas of companionship seeking.

"Fortune favors the bold," she mused, her mind alight with epiphanies of love's labyrinthine landscapes. For indeed, the app had become more than a mere platform; it was a community tapestry, interlaced with the threads of shared humanity, each narrative a testament to the resilience of the heart and the indomitable will to find one's co-conspirator in the capricious escapade that is life.

Sarah and Mark, each shepherding a small hand within their own, approached the entrance of the local aquarium—a kaleidoscopic castle where marine life danced behind glassy ramparts. The decision to introduce their children in such an environment was a meticulously crafted stratagem, calculated to foster interaction through shared wonder rather than the pressure of direct engagement. It was an undertaking that bore the weight of parental hope like a fragile seashell cradling the sound of future seas.

"Look, Mommy! Fishies!" exclaimed Sarah's daughter, her cherubic face alight with unbridled enthusiasm as they crossed the threshold into the underwater realm. Mark's son, slightly older and ensconced in the quiet fortitude that often accompanies youth is first brushes with responsibility, offered a timid smile in agreement. Their expressions, though differing in intensity, were united in their innocence—a tableau vivant of childhood's unjaded curiosity.

As the quartet meandered through the dimly lit corridors, flanked by tanks that teemed with aquatic life, Sarah saw the children's reactions with a perspicacity that only motherhood could hone. The tentative glances exchanged between the two youngsters, punctuated by moments of shared laughter at the antics of a particularly gregarious octopus, bespoke an emerging camaraderie that transcended their initial reticence. Indeed, the vibrant tapestries of coral and the languid ballet of jellyfish served as silent arbitrators in this delicate dance of new acquaintances.

Meanwhile, beyond the confines of their maritime excursion, the tendrils of Sarah's influence had woven themselves into the fabric of her support group. Emboldened by her narrative of cautious optimism, her fellow single parents cast their nets into the digital sea, buoyed by the prospect of discovering a catch that would complement their solitary journeys. As they recounted tales of their own fledgling connections, laughter and empathetic nods crisscrossed the coffee-stained tables at their weekly gatherings, each anecdote a mosaic piece contributing to a larger portrait of hope rekindled.

"Can you believe it? He enjoys my baking disasters," chortled one
of the group members, her voice a lilting symphony of newfound
joy that resonated within the collective consciousness of the
assembly. Another, his eyes shimmering with the kind of shy pride
that accompanies unexpected fortune, added, "She didn't bat an
eye when I told her about my son's reptile obsession. In fact, she
suggested we all visit the zoo together."

These vignettes, once mere hypotheticals whispered amidst
hushed tones of uncertainty, now rang out with the clarity of truth
realized. Each story served as both beacon and affirmation,
illuminating paths previously shrouded by doubt's insidious fog. It
became apparent that Sarah's foray into the world of virtual
courtship had inadvertently sown seeds that blossomed into a
garden of collective experience—a verdant expanse where
laughter mingled with revelations, and trepidation gave way to the
tender shoots of burgeoning romance.

And so, with each step taken beneath the azure glow of the
aquarium's vaulted chambers, Sarah's heart swelled not only with
the nascent bonds forming before her very eyes but also with the
knowledge that her journey had become a catalyst for others. With
every shared glance between her daughter and Mark's son, and
with every testimonial uttered in her support group's sanctum, the
symphony of connection crescendo to a resounding ode to the
bravery inherent in seeking companionship amidst the
unpredictable tides of single parenthood.

In the labyrinthine dance of blending families, where steps often
misalign and melodies clash, Sarah and Mark navigated their
burgeoning relationship with a grace born of mutual respect and
the unspoken vows of open-hearted transparency. The challenges
they faced were manifold—a mélange of schedules, emotions, and
histories colliding in a kaleidoscope of modern family dynamics—
but it was their steadfast commitment to communication that kept
the entropy at bay. With each new layer of domestic intricacy
unfurling before them, they approached every discussion as co-
conspirators, wielding empathy as both shield and beacon.

As autumn ushered in its tapestry of fiery hues and the whisper of winter's chill began to find its voice within the rustling leaves, Sarah found herself cocooned within a reflective reprieve. She pondered her journey, an odyssey that had charted a course through the treacherous straits of skepticism to the fertile shores of companionship. Gratitude blossomed within her, its roots entwined around the bedrock of the app—a digital Cupid's bow that had launched arrows with unerring precision, piercing the armor of loneliness she had donned in the wake of her divorce— and the support group, a constellation of kindred spirits whose own tales of love rediscovered served as a testament to the power of vulnerability.

Her heart, once guarded behind the battlements of caution, now throbbed with the fullness of shared affection, and with it came an evangelist's zeal. Sarah became a herald for the cautious yet courageous hearts seeking solace in the arms of another, urging them to arm themselves with prudence while daring to traverse the tightrope of intimacy that online dating so peculiarly presented. Her words, imbued with the wisdom of experience, became a clarion call to those navigating the pixelated sea of profiles: remain vigilant, prioritize safety, but let not fear become the jailer of your desires.

In the quietude of evening, as the last vestiges of twilight surrendered to the symphony of stars above, Sarah allowed herself a moment of contemplation. The digital realm—once a foreign country marked by the unknown—had yielded a harvest rich with the promise of tomorrow. Emboldened by the love she had found and the success stories echoing within her circle, she championed the potential nestled within calculated risks, her narrative a mosaic of resilience and hope etched into the annals of modern romance.

The horizon, an artist's masterstroke of crimson and gold, seemed to conspire with the universe, painting a perfect backdrop for two silhouettes clasping hands as if to declare their unwavering commitment. Sarah, with her dark hair now caught in the gentle embrace of the evening zephyr, held onto Mark's hand, her fingers entwined with him in a silent language that spoke volumes of trust and shared tomorrows. The tender but firm grip was the culmination of countless moments, a mosaic of text messages, heartfelt conversations, and the delicate dance of new love crafted within the digital tapestry of a modern age.

Mark, whose presence had become as reassuring to Sarah as the steadfast lighthouse to the mariner amid tempestuous seas, matched her step by step, his own journey through the labyrinth of single parenthood now intertwined with hers. His eyes, reflecting the last embers of daylight, carried the sheen of a man who had stumbled, risen, and found himself walking beside a woman whose resilience shimmered like the very stars taking their places above.

As they advanced, the soft crunch of gravel beneath their steps became a rhythmic ode to the perseverance that had ushered them to this juncture. Each footfall was a testament to the calculated risks they had embraced, the very act of placing one's heart into the hands of another, across the digital divide—a stark reminder that fortitude in love often requires embracing the very vulnerabilities that once prompted barricades.

Their laughter, light yet laden with the depth of shared understanding, punctuated the tranquility of the evening, betraying the gravity of their mutual odyssey. It was a sound that resonated with the subtleties of hope and the acknowledgement that even amidst the plethora of swipes and notifications, authenticity could be unearthed, and kindred spirits discovered.

Indeed, as they ambled together toward the impending nightfall, Sarah and Mark were not merely two figures against the waning light but emissaries of possibility, embodiments of what happens when the heart dares to author its next chapter, when it chooses to write a narrative where caution and courage waltz in harmonious balance.

Thus, with every step into the fading glow of day's end, the couple personified the triumph of an app designed to unite, of support.

groups that fortified, and of love rekindled in the digital hearth. Their shadows, elongating on the ground behind them, were not marks of darkness but rather elongated heralds of the light that lay ahead—their journey, a poignant illustration of life's unfaltering potential for renewal at the crossroads of technology and human connection.

About the Author

Tory Swedlund may be a newcomer to the world of authors, but his passion for writing has been a constant companion for years. He pours his thoughts onto journal pages, using them as a tool to process life's ups and downs. It is through this practice that he has crafted some of the most captivating and imaginative storylines in the literary world.

But Tory's talents go beyond his writing abilities. As a single father of two young girls, aged 10 and 7, he juggles his responsibilities with grace and determination. And though it may seem like an impossible feat, Tory is also a recovering alcoholic and drug addict who has been sober for an astonishing 24 years. Perhaps it is his journey to sobriety that gives him the insight and strength to create such compelling stories.

Stay connected with Tory as he continues to unleash his imagination through upcoming books like "Final Swipe" and "Eating Death". With so much life experience under his belt, there is no doubt that Tory has many more amazing tales waiting to be told.

www.ingramcontent.com/pod-product-compliance
Lightning Source LLC
Chambersburg PA
CBHW080006180726
48002CB00021B/3123